Julianne wa
leaned dow
his daughter's forehead.

Julianne looked away and swallowed hard. She had to get out of here, out of this house soon, or she'd make a complete fool of herself by crying over things she couldn't explain. Then she felt Luke's hand touch her shoulder, and she raised her tear-filled eyes to meet his understanding gaze. He moved closer, easing her into his arms, where she let go of the sorrow as she buried her face against his chest and wept.

How long they'd stood there, Julianne wasn't sure. But when she was finished crying, she raised her head and instantly missed the steady beating of his heart against her ear.

"I'm sorry, Luke. I didn't mean to cry. I don't even...I don't even know you well enough to fall apart in front of you like that." Julianne's words were rambling, and she knew it. She was grateful when Luke raised a hand, touching his index finger to her lips.

"Julianne." He whispered her lovely name in the stillness of the evening before his mouth brushed hers in a hesitant first kiss.

Books by Kathryn Alexander

Love Inspired

The Reluctant Bride #18

A Wedding in the Family #42

The Forever Husband #78

Twin Wishes #96

KATHRYN ALEXANDER

writes inspirational romance because, having been a Christian for many years, incorporating the element of faith in the Lord into a romantic story line seemed like a lovely and appropriate idea. After all, in a society where love for a lifetime is difficult to find, imagine discovering it, unexpectedly, as a gift sent from God.

Kathryn is married to Kelly, her own personal love of a lifetime. She and her husband have one son, John, who is the proud owner of the family's two house pests, Herbie the cat and Copper the dog.

For nearly five years Kathryn and her family have been members of their church, where she co-teaches a Sunday school class of active two-year-olds. She is now a stay-at-home mom who writes between car pooling, baby-sitting and applying bandages when necessary.

Twin Wishes
Kathryn Alexander

Published by Steeple Hill Books™

Special thanks and acknowledgment are given to Kathryn Alexander for her contribution to the Fairweather miniseries.

STEEPLE HILL BOOKS

Steeple
Hill™

ISBN 0-373-87102-3

TWIN WISHES

Visit us at www.steeplehill.com

Printed in U.S.A.

Be still, and know that I am God: I will be exalted among the heathen, I will be exalted in the earth.
—*Psalms* 46:10

To my father, Olan Tussing,
who died New Year's Day, 1999.
Dad, you are dearly loved and sadly missed.

Chapter One

"Julianne, I'd like you to meet two new students. This is Nora and this—" the woman speaking reached behind her to pull a young brown-haired, blue-eyed boy from his hiding place "—this is Todd."

Julianne Quinn knelt down to eye-level with the children in the doorway of her classroom at the day-care center. "So, you must be four years old if you're going to be in my class," she said softly. With a gentle movement, she touched the pink cheek of little Nora.

"You smell good," the girl commented, staring into the pretty brown eyes of her new teacher. Julianne smiled back and thanked her.

"We're twins, Nora and me," the boy stated as if giving official notice of something that was already quite obvious to Julianne.

"Well, you *do* look a lot alike," she replied. "And

you're the same size and age. Yep, I'd have to agree with you. You must be twins." Julianne tousled Todd's light brown hair with a soft touch. "C'mon in and I'll let you meet the other children."

But before Julianne could stand up, Nora rushed toward her, throwing her arms around her neck and holding on as if for dear life. Julianne slipped her arms around the child in a firm hug while she watched Todd gravitate back toward the woman who had brought them into the center today—his aunt, Maggie Wren—the next person to speak.

"And this is my brother, Luke O'Hara," she introduced the tall, dark-haired man standing next to her.

Julianne stood up, scooping Nora up into her arms as she did so and came face-to-face with the man she'd already heard so much about from her friend, Maggie. Julianne smiled and extended a slender hand to greet him. "Nice to meet you, Mr. O'Hara," she offered.

Luke O'Hara responded, without smiling. "You, too, Miss Quinn." He looked past Julianne into the brightly colored classroom, complete with chairs and desks in primary colors, cubbyholes and shelves, toys and puzzles, and dark blue mats for nap time, he assumed. It seemed to him like a friendly enough environment for his children; but, still, if his sister Maggie didn't work at this day-care center, he would hesitate leaving them in an unfamiliar setting with a stranger for a teacher. Luke glanced at Nora and Todd. The protest he'd expected from the kids hadn't started yet. That surprised him. Usually the mere mention of being left someplace, anyplace, while Luke went to work made them whine and plead so that he could barely leave the house. That was one reason he had made the decision to move here to live closer to his sister, the only real family he had left since his wife's death last year. He needed Maggie's help with the children.

"Luke, I think the children are going to be fine here, if you want to leave now,' Maggie stated as she saw Todd turn from her and move back toward Julianne, who was still holding his sister. "I'll be right down the hallway if they need me."

Luke looked skeptical, Julianne surmised as she watched his eyebrows draw together in a doubtful frown. His face reminded her a little of his sister, with the same dark brown hair and striking blue eyes as Maggie; but Luke was much taller, broad-shouldered and quieter, sadder than his sunny-dispositioned sibling. And better looking than Maggie had indicated. Sisters sometimes embellish the truth at times in describing a brother they love. With three brothers of her own, Julianne knew that all too well. But, if anything, Maggie had understated the facts about Luke, except for his countenance. The look on his face revealed his melancholy feelings, and his mouth was straight and unyielding. Julianne thought briefly it would be nice to see that mouth smile. It could take years off his face, and might even lighten the load of grief he quietly carried.

She reached for Todd's small hand, and he allowed her to clasp it warmly in her own. "Let's go look at Noah's ark, and then we'll have a snack while you get to know the other kids.'' She nodded at the four other children playing with a large toy ark in the middle of the room. Plastic animals were scattered around everywhere on the huge braided rug they were sitting on. Julianne hoped Luke would leave soon, before the twins decided they didn't want him to go. She had a sinking feeling they could burst into teary-eyed protests at any moment.

''I need to go to Minneapolis this morning to look over a job site for a landscaping project I've accepted. I probably can't be back here until around four-thirty.'' Luke glanced from his sister back to Julianne Quinn. He hadn't really looked at her when he had first entered the room. He'd been too concerned about the children's reaction to their new surroundings, but now he noticed she was tall, blond and had friendly brown eyes. And he had a business to run. ''Is four-thirty too late to pick them up?'' he asked.

''No, that would be fine,'' Julianne responded. ''We'll be open until six.'' She smiled at him, but he didn't return the gesture.

Luke turned and quickly exited the room. That seemed the wisest thing to do since the kids were momentarily distracted by the toys and other children. He felt guilty for leaving them like that. No hugs, no goodbyes. But he knew it was the better choice. Anytime they said goodbye to him now, they cried. It was almost as if each time he left, they thought they might never see him again. And Luke sympathized with them, knowing they had reason to be afraid. That's what had happened with their mother. Luke had taken her to the hospital, and she had not returned home. But that had been months ago. Fourteen to be exact. Luke exhaled a long sigh as he climbed into the dark blue pickup with O'Hara's Landscaping printed in white lettering on both doors. Today, a hot summer day in July, marked a pivotal point in their lives, although the twins were too young to understand its significance. This was a new day in a new community and, maybe, just maybe, a new beginning for Luke and his children. If only he could loosen his grip on the past.

Julianne's first day with the children was a rather uneventful one compared to what she'd expected. The twins stayed close to each other most of the time. She'd had to break up a squabble or two between them before lunchtime, but that wasn't anything out of the ordinary for four-year-olds, she knew too well. Aunt Maggie stopped in several times during the day to check on her niece and nephew, but they waved at her and went on with their play. The only problem Julianne encountered was nap time which followed the lunch hour. Nora cried when Julianne switched off the lights although the room still had plenty of light from the sun sifting through the polka-dot curtains. Julianne sat down on one of the blue mats next to Nora and put her arm around the little girl. Within two seconds, Todd scooted over by her on the other side and nestled snugly into her other arm. The other children in the room all rested on their mats as was their normal routine during this time of the day. But neither Nora nor Todd slept a wink. They remained cuddled up by Julianne for the entire hour, fighting a gallant and victorious battle against the sandman. The two were quiet most of the time, only occasionally saying something to Julianne, who had asked them not to disturb the other children. When the rest period ended, Nora returned to coloring the picture of kittens she'd been working on earlier, saying to Todd, "I told you she wasn't going away."

Julianne went on with story time, having all the children gather around in a circle on the worn braided rug to listen to her read. She couldn't help but wonder how helpless Nora and Todd must have felt when their mother slipped away from them. Maggie had told Julianne about Kimberly O'Hara and how leukemia had taken her life last year. The Lord had helped Luke and the kids through the tragedy Maggie had explained, although Luke hadn't seen it that way. He'd given up on his faith entirely after his wife's death. The only remaining connection between himself and the church was his attempt to get the kids there when he could. Kimberly had asked him to promise to raise the children as Christians. That was one of the reasons he had moved to Fairweather, Minnesota this summer—to be near his sister Maggie and her husband Frank, both dedicated Christians who would help him try to keep his promise to Kimberly. As for himself, Luke didn't believe in much of anything anymore except hard work and honesty. Admirable qualities, his sister had acknowledged, but hardly sufficient for raising a family. Maggie was quick to point out that Luke needed more. He needed the Lord, he needed to stop letting his work turn him into an "absentee" parent and, Maggie believed, he needed a wife who could help point him in the right direction. And Julianne Quinn would know which direction was right.

When four-thirty finally arrived that first day, Luke returned to the center to pick up his children, and he wasn't surprised when Nora and Todd came running, shrieking with delight into his arms after a long day apart. Luke wore new blue jeans and a short-sleeved work shirt of light gray, neither of which were dirty since he had done little manual labor in the past eight hours. He had inspected a job site and purchased necessary supplies to begin the project in Minneapolis tomorrow. Then he had discussed his plans with the three college kids his brother-in-law, Frank Wren, had lined up for him as temporary help. They'd each been in the Book-Stop Frank owned and mentioned they were looking for summer work. Frank told them about Luke's landscaping business and the need for a couple of extra pairs of hands in the coming weeks. The boys were exactly the help Luke was looking for, and they agreed to work for a reasonable sum. With most of his mental to-do list for the day accomplished, he was glad to get back to the twins and find out how Maggie's day-care center was working out for them. If he couldn't get the kids settled into some kind of an acceptable routine, Fairweather might not turn out to be much of an improvement over the suburbs of Chicago. Luke had higher hopes than that.

"Well, it looks like they're glad to see their father,'' Julianne remarked as she watched Luke gather both children into his arms for a hearty hug. "They've been watching for you from the side window for the past two hours."

"Did they do okay today?" Luke asked, glancing from his kids into Julianne's gentle brown eyes. He suddenly thought that she looked like she was meant for this job—spending her days caring for children.

"They did very well," she answered and reached for the red-striped backpack Maggie had left for them. "We did need Fluffy and Dunkum, from time to time for some comforting. I'm glad you packed their stuffed animals in this bag." Julianne thought of the crying spell Nora and Todd had both experienced in midafternoon. Too much newness for their four-year-old spirits to absorb. "New home, new place, new teacher. It's a lot for them to adjust to."

Luke's frown was an immediate overreaction. He needed this arrangement to work and any hint that it might not, didn't sit well with him. "Didn't Maggie check on them?"

Just then, Maggie entered the door behind her brother and placed her hand on his shoulder. "Yes, I checked on these little characters several times, Luke, and they were absolutely fine. Nothing to worry about at all. Just ask their teacher."

Julianne nodded in agreement. "They really were okay, Mr. O'Hara. I think they had some fun today. I hope you'll bring them back tomorrow."

"He will," Maggie answered for her brother, which turned his frown into something close to a smile. "He has to because this is where I'll be."

"You're hard to argue with, Maggie." Luke released the children from a hug, and they immediately began complaining. Their favorite place lately seemed to be in their father's embrace. "C'mon, kids. Let's go have supper." He extended an arm to accept the backpack from Julianne. "Nora and Todd will be here around seven-thirty in the morning. Thanks for taking care of them today."

"You're welcome. I'll look forward to seeing them tomorrow. Bye, Nora. Bye, Todd. See you in the morning." She looked at Luke with questioning eyes. "And, Fluffy and Dunkum...don't forget to bring them, too."

Luke nodded and guided the children and their stuffed animals toward the doorway. "Thank you, Miss Quinn...and Maggie, I'll see you tomorrow."

"Do you want to come over for dinner tonight?" Maggie offered before the trio disappeared through the door.

"Some other time, thanks. I have some figures to go over tonight while the kids are having their meat loaf and mashed potatoes," Luke responded, and then they were off, into the truck and on their way to the two-story, older home Luke had purchased not far from Frank and Maggie's place.

"He can cook meat loaf and mashed potatoes?" Julianne repeated. "Is he serious?"

Maggie remarked. "Yes, he's serious...as long as the local supermarket carries frozen dinners. I swear, I think that's about all those children eat anymore."

Julianne thought of her own freezer stacked full of packaged entrees. "Maybe that's not so bad, Maggie.

At least they're eating their vegetables in some way other than French fries.''

But Maggie shook her head. "They should have better than that. Luke and I grew up on home-cooked meals.'' Then she offered a laugh as she took a quick glance at the extra pounds she'd carried for years that had nothing to do with her progressing pregnancy. "Of course, I guess I look like I'm well fed, don't I?''

"You look beautiful,'' Julianne responded and gave her friend a heartfelt hug. "That's one of the benefits of being pregnant.''

A benefit Julianne knew she herself might never know—if her doctor was correct. She swallowed back her resurfacing sadness and looked toward the two remaining little girls sitting happily on the braided rug in the middle of the room, trying to put large pieces of a puzzle together. How could God let her go through life without a child to love?

The next hour and a half passed slowly until, finally, the last of the parents picked up their children, and Julianne was free to leave. She pulled off her brown flats and replaced them with jogging shoes— her favorites. Then she waved to the director of the day-care center, Betty Anderson, as she paused by her office on the way to the front door.

"Waiting on Warren to pick you up?'' Julianne asked.

Betty adjusted her small half-moon reading glasses on her nose. "Yes, we're going down to Olaf's Deli for soup and sandwiches.''

Betty was a widow who had only recently begun

seeing someone after five years alone, and everyone at the center was happy for her. The new man in Betty's life, Warren Sinclair, picked her up frequently at the end of her workday so they could have dinner together. Julianne had seen them leave together many times, and had, on occasion, wished she'd found someone to share soup and a sandwich with, too. Since she'd broken up with her college boyfriend, she'd been mostly alone. Too alone, she realized. Not all men were the weak, selfish human beings her old boyfriend had proven to be. She knew too many men of integrity to think that way. Reverend Benjamin Hunter, for one. They had dated briefly some time ago. Although it was always nice to find a new friend, they quickly agreed that friendship was all they had found since the romantic chemistry between them was lacking, leaving Julianne to soup and sandwiches alone again.

"Have a good time," she said to Betty before heading out the front door of the newly renovated two-story building that was located next door to the church. Julianne pushed her blond hair away from her face as a welcome gust of wind blew over her. This July had been a warm one but Julianne still preferred walking to and from the center rather than driving. It was only a few short blocks to her apartment. She rented the upstairs of an old rambling house owned by Fairweather's postmaster, and the home was located not far from the south side of the town green. On Julianne's way home, she passed by the deli where Betty and Warren would soon be enjoying their dinner, then Frank and Maggie Wren's

Book-Stop which was a combination bookstore and café, Swenson's Bakery and Peter's Ice Cream Parlor, to name a few of the businesses that lined the path between home and work.

By the time Julianne reached the twentieth step and turned the key in the lock of her silent apartment, her stomach was already growling. She placed her keys on the hook beside the door and headed toward her bedroom where she quickly slipped out of her jogging shoes as well as her long summer dress of pale blues and browns. Tan shorts, a green T-shirt and bare feet felt much nicer as she walked across the cool kitchen floor to pull open the door of her refrigerator. Nothing promising caught her eye. "Why didn't I stop at Olaf's Deli or Frank's Book-Stop, or somewhere, and buy something good for supper?" Then she opened the freezer. The frozen dinner on top was her pick of the evening. "Well, Nora and Todd," she said aloud to herself as she tossed the red box into the trash can and slid the paper tray into the microwave, "I guess meat loaf and mashed potatoes are on my menu tonight, too."

Several blocks away, Luke O'Hara discarded three paper trays and poured leftover chocolate milk from red-and-blue cups into the sink, wondering why neither of his children ever seemed to finish drinking their milk. He'd reminded them again and again to do so with no success; but he'd learned by now that he had to pick his battles, and this didn't seem a worthy one.

"Daddy, can we go see Julianne again tomorrow?'' Nora was asking as she came running into the kitchen carrying her pink bunny. ''Todd and me like her.''

''I'm glad you do, hon,'' Luke replied as he placed the dirty silverware and cups into the dishwasher. He'd become fairly quick about loading the appliance, with practice, especially for someone who'd rarely set foot inside the kitchen before his wife had passed away. ''I'll be taking you there in the morning so you can spend the day with her. And Aunt Maggie will be at the center, too, if you need her.'' He looked down into his little girl's sweet face and reached out to touch her cheek as his heart flooded with emotion. He stood silently amazed that he could feel such love for anyone with this heart that, most times, felt cold as stone.

''Nora!'' Todd called out his sister's name from somewhere beyond the kitchen. Probably the staircase to their upstairs bedrooms Luke estimated from the faintness of his voice. The apartment they'd left behind had been one level, so the idea of steps to climb captivated their interest. They used any excuse they could find to go up and down the polished oak staircase, running their little hands down the wooden railing on each and every trip.

''Coooming, Todd,'' Nora called out. Then she turned and ran from her father's touch, and Luke was almost relieved. If she'd have stood there a moment longer, looking up at him with that baby-blue gaze, his own stinging eyes might have teared up. And Luke O'Hara hadn't allowed that to happen in a very long time.

So, with the ever faithful Fluffy tucked under one arm, Nora scampered off to join her brother. Luke glanced at his watch. It was 6:00 p.m. Time to watch the news, if he could get away with it. He switched on the small television set on top of the refrigerator, carefully leaving the volume down low so the kids couldn't hear. Stories that involved sirens, ambulances…anything about death or violence upset Todd and Nora, so Luke had mostly taken to reading the morning newspaper to gather his news of the day. But there were those occasions when he could watch part of the broadcast without the children being aware of it. Like now. The weather forecast for the week said that there would be a string of warm days, with only an occasional passing shower, right into the Fourth of July. Maggie had insisted that Luke promise to bring the children to her house for the holiday and join her church in its annual picnic on the green that afternoon. And it sounded like the weather would be ideal for such an outing.

Julianne switched off the radio in her kitchen after listening to the news and weather and then reached for the pitcher of iced tea. "The Fourth of July is supposed to be a beautiful day, Goldie," she said to the fish that was swimming around in its oversize bowl on a nearby counter. "And I'm counting on you to still be here to enjoy it." The tea poured quietly into her glass as she studied the small orange fish. An ordinary goldfish, Maggie had warned. The kind that never lasts long, she'd said when she and

Julianne had peered into the fish tank in the corner of the Fairweather Variety Store.

"Ordinary," Julianne remarked with a shake of her head. "How could Maggie call you that? Didn't she notice that beautiful flowing tail of yours?" she asked out loud. "And it's been three days since I brought you home from the store, and you're doing fine so far." Though not without the purchase of a second, much larger bowl, a small air filter for a sum of twenty dollars, and a certain amount of prayer.

Julianne's luck with pets was not the best, so she was determined to keep this one alive as long as possible. The hungry little stray dog she'd taken in last winter had been hit by a car one morning several months ago, and the kitten that a teaching assistant from the center had given her disappeared recently on one of his daily outings. That evening, Julianne had remained on the top of the landing outside her apartment for hours, waiting for the kitten to come home. She'd balanced her checkbook, paid her monthly bills and written letters to all three of her brothers on that warm spring evening as she watched for his return. But he didn't come back. By the time she stood up to go inside, Julianne's bottom was nearly numb from sitting in one position so long. That's when she'd decided—no more pets! And she'd stuck to her decision until this week. Until she stood in the variety store, in front of the bubbling fish tank with Goldie's big bulging eyes staring right into her own lonely brown ones. Maybe one more try with a different kind of pet wouldn't be so bad, she'd decided. And Goldie would be someone to come home to…kind of.

Julianne reached into the cupboard over the sink to pull out a bag of chocolate chip cookies and ate a handful of them without counting. Losing pets was nothing compared to losing someone. Little Nora and Todd crossed her mind for the umpteenth time since she'd returned home. How very young they were to let go of their mother. "Lord, if I can help them in some way," she breathed the prayer, "then use me to do so, I pray. Help me to be comforting, loving, nurturing…whatever it is those kids need while they're with me. Lead me and guide me to know what to do, what to say, when to hold them, when not to… You know I need Your help with these two children more than any of the others in my class, Lord. Please help me." And He would, Julianne was certain as she put the sack of cookies away. She'd learned to trust God more over the past year than she ever had before. He'd helped her through the miserable breakup with her longtime boyfriend.

Julianne sighed as she headed toward the bathroom to gather up her dirty clothes for her weekly trip to the laundromat. She'd almost married Craig Johnson. It sent shivers down her spine to think how close she'd come to trusting her future to a man with so little compassion. Where had her own good judgment disappeared to?

The bag of laundry Julianne lifted was not heavy since it was filled with mostly lightweight summer outfits. With the detergent and fabric softener she needed waiting in the basket, she slipped her feet into a pair of leather sandals and was ready to go.

Thank the Lord, Craig had dumped her, Julianne thought and then gave a soft laugh. If he hadn't, she might have blundered ahead into a marriage that wouldn't have worked. And then, what? She wondered momentarily. No husband, no children... What would she have done?

She picked up her canvas purse, tossed it into the basket and headed for the front door. What would she have done? She wasn't sure what the answer to that question might be, but she *was* certain she'd have found one, sooner or later, with the Lord's help. She always had in the past...in every way except one. And she was confident, even in that area of her life, an answer would come. Just because she couldn't see the solution now, didn't mean it wasn't there. She trusted her life to the Lord completely. He'd guided her through many difficulties, saved her from a life with Craig and He would make it clear, at some point, how she was supposed to move ahead to the life she wanted...even without the ability to have children. But for now, she had work to do. Pushing her hair back over her shoulder, she headed toward Fairweather's only laundromat. She wouldn't worry about being lonely tonight. There was always someone to talk with while the machines were running.

Luke finished cleaning up the kitchen and went to the living room to check on the twins, who were noisily playing with Nora's large plastic kitchen set.

Just as Luke stepped into the room, he saw Nora pick up a plastic toy spatula and hit Todd on the head with it. Todd whirled around, swinging at his sister and the fight was on.

"Whoa, kids. No fighting. You know the rules," Luke said as he separated the two with an easy movement. "Nora, tell Todd you're sorry for hitting him."

"No!" she answered. "He took my job. I was rinsing the dishes in the sink until he pushed me away."

"I just wanted to do what Dad was doing," Todd yelled his reply. "He was in the kitchen washing dishes. That should have been my job."

Luke shook his head. "Anyone can rinse the dishes. Dad, mom, boy, girl…it doesn't matter. Everyone needs to take a turn. That's the part you need to learn. Taking turns. Now, Nora—"

"No!" she shouted and ran toward the staircase. "It's my job. A girl's job. A mom's job!"

Luke watched her go, letting her run up the steps by herself as she ran to her room. He placed a hand across his mouth and lowered his head in a moment of complete frustration. He knew exactly what Nora meant. Kimberly had been responsible for "kitchen duty," as he used to call it. It had only become Luke's job out of necessity.

"Come on, Todd. Let's go upstairs and talk to Nora." Father and son climbed the steps slowly, hand in hand. Comforting his children hadn't gotten much easier with time, and Luke wished he could reach a point where he felt he was good at it. Or adequate, at least. Then there were those times when

Luke wished he had someone to comfort him. The Lord he'd turned his back on was his best hope for that, he knew, but he was still too angry to look to his Heavenly Father for help. God hadn't answered his last prayer the way Luke had wanted. He'd found no reason to think anything would be different this time.

"Reverend Ben. How nice to see you," Julianne said as she looked up from folding clean towels.

Reverend Benjamin Hunter smiled. "Good to see you, Julianne. Laundry night for you, too?" He reached into his pocket for coins.

"Afraid so," she answered. "But I thought the church board voted to have a washer and dryer placed in the parsonage for you."

Ben nodded. "They did, but they just haven't gotten around to it yet." Quarters clinked into the washer closest to where Ben was standing. "So, how's everything with you, Julianne? We missed you in service last week."

"I have an 'excused absence,'" Julianne offered with a smile. "I was in Minneapolis visiting one of my brothers. He's getting married soon, and this will probably be the last chance I have to spend a weekend with him—just the two of us."

"Well, I hope you had a good time," Ben remarked. He dumped a basketful of clothes into a second machine. "We had someone new with us last Sunday. Maggie's brother Luke and his twins were there." He closed the lid and glanced toward Julianne who was busy stacking clean clothes into her basket. "I thought of you."

Startled, Julianne stopped what she was doing and met Ben's gaze. "Me? Why?"

Ben grinned. "Probably because Maggie had mentioned to me a time or two—or more—that you could be just what Luke's children need right now."

"They're in my class at the center," Julianne acknowledged. "Today was their first day."

"How'd it go?"

She shrugged. "Okay, I think. They let their father leave for work this morning without any tantrums. That was a very good sign." Julianne returned to stacking her laundry and then gathered up her belongings, including the latest romance novel she had just finished. "They seemed to genuinely like me."

"I can't imagine anyone feeling otherwise," Ben commented before taking a seat in a nearby chair. "But I want you to be careful, Julianne." He paused. "The O'Hara children's needs are great, and I know what a nurturing, giving soul you naturally tend to be. I'm worried you'll be hurt."

"I love all the children in my class. Nora and Todd O'Hara will be no different."

"They are very different. Nora and Todd need a mother," Ben corrected. "None of your other kids fall into that category. And Luke O'Hara may not be ready for another relationship. I know how badly you want children, Julianne, and I believe the Lord will work that out for you, somehow, in time. But give Him time, don't rush ahead."

"If you and I didn't already know we weren't exactly meant for each other, I'd think you were jealous, Reverend Benjamin Hunter,'' Julianne teased.

"I'm just worried about you," he replied.

"I'm not interested in becoming the next Mrs. O'Hara, if that's what you're thinking," she assured him with a disbelieving shake of her head, her blond hair swishing gently against her neck. What would make Ben think such a thing? "And I'm not considering kidnapping Nora and Todd to keep them for my own, for heaven's sake. They're just two kids in my class, and I'll do the best I can for them during the hours I'm with them." She scooped up her basket and belongings. "From the way you've been talking, I suspect you're the one who's been reading the romance novels." She grinned at him in amusement.

Reverend Ben shook his head and gave a quiet laugh. "No, I'll leave those to you. But think about what I've said."

Julianne agreed with a nod. Then she headed toward the double doors to exit the laundromat. "Thank you, Ben. I'll talk to you later." She'd probably see him the next day at the center, she knew. Most days she did run into him since Reverend Ben and the day-care center shared a secretary by the name of Emma Fulton. Now, there was someone who would love the book Julianne had just finished reading. But Julianne wasn't sure she wanted to put any more notions of romance in Emma's head than were already floating around in there. The woman had done everything in her power to throw Julianne and Reverend Ben together some months ago since Emma had decided that Julianne would make a perfect pastor's wife. Ben and Julianne had finally gone out together and discovered that what each had found was a new friend. Nothing more. But that date with Reverend Ben had helped Julianne get over her fiancé, and she soon decided she was ready to try a new relationship—whenever the right person came along. And, so far, he hadn't appeared. Or, if he had, she hadn't recognized him as such.

A short time later, Julianne climbed the stairs to her apartment as quickly as she could, considering her arms were full with a basket of clothes. She'd heard the phone ringing from the sidewalk below.

"Hello, yes," she answered, nearly out of breath after grabbing up the phone. "This is Julianne Quinn. Who's calling, please?"

"This is Luke O'Hara…Maggie's brother," came the reply.

Chapter Two

Julianne let her laundry basket drop to the floor. Why would he be calling her? At home like this? "Yes, Mr. O'Hara, is something wrong?"

"No, but I just spoke with my brother-in-law, Frank Wren, and he suggested I call you since Maggie wasn't available. He gave me your number. I hope you don't mind."

"No, that's fine. I don't mind. How can I help you?"

"I was wondering if I could drop off the kids earlier in the morning than originally planned?"

"Well, yes," Julianne replied. "I'll be there early. What time did you have in mind?"

"Around seven? Would that be okay?"

"Yes. That's fine. I'll be looking for you...for the kids, I mean. Thank you for calling."

Their conversation ended, and Julianne sat down, sinking into the nearby sofa. Thank you for calling?

"What a stupid thing to say," she lamented aloud to no one but herself. "He called to ask me a question about the center, and I acted like I was grateful for the opportunity to speak with him." She got up and walked into the kitchen to get a cold soda from the refrigerator.

"What do you think, Goldie? Have I been listening to Reverend Ben and Maggie too much? Everybody seems to expect me to fall for this guy. I'd better be careful or they'll have me believing it, too."

"Maggie!" Julianne called out as she saw Frank Wren dropping off his wife in front of the center early the next morning. "Wait up!" She ran the last block to catch up with her friend.

"Good thing you wear those running shoes," Maggie remarked, glancing down at the sneakers that clashed with the pale pink blouse and gray skirt that Julianne wore. "You couldn't move that fast in heels."

"Maggie, why did Frank tell your brother to call me last night? He could have easily answered any question Luke had about the daily schedule here at the center. Luke didn't need me—"

"Oh, he needs you, Julianne. He just doesn't know it yet." Maggie smiled. "Today's going to be a beautiful day, don't you think?"

"C'mon, Maggie," Julianne responded. "You're starting to remind me of Emma Fulton. Your brother and I barely know each other's names, let alone the idea of anything more. He doesn't need me, I don't need him and I wish you, Reverend Ben and anyone else who thinks we might be interested in each other—''

"Reverend Ben?'' Maggie interrupted. "What did he have to say about all of this?''

"Nothing. Nothing important, anyway,'' Julianne replied. "Maggie, please don't force this thing. It's awkward, it's uncomfortable.'' And that was only the beginning of how odd it felt. The whole idea of being interested in some man she'd met only yesterday seemed unbelievable.

Maggie looped her arm through Julianne's as they walked together up the front sidewalk to the center. The patriotic wind catcher of red, white and blue that Maggie had put up yesterday flapped in the early morning breeze. "I don't want to push too hard, Julianne. I really don't. But I just have a feeling that you and Luke—''

"Now you really do sound like Emma Fulton. Remember how anxious she was to pair me up with Reverend Ben?'' Julianne stopped walking. "It just doesn't work that way. Forget about 'fixing me up' with the first eligible man that comes along, and quit trying to solve your brother's problems for him. People need space, Maggie. We need to solve our own problems, find our own way through life. I'm sure Luke would say that he feels the same if you took the time to ask him.''

But Maggie wasn't asking. Or listening, apparently. "So, did the two of you have a nice conversation on the phone last night?''

Julianne groaned in frustration. "Are you paying attention to anything that I'm saying?'' she asked her friend before turning to continue their walk to the front door.

"I will pay attention if you tell me something good about your talk with Luke."

"The only good thing about it was that it didn't last long. It was awkward and unnecessary. Frank could have told Luke he could bring the kids in earlier than he planned without my input on the matter. You know that."

Two cars pulled into the parking area beside the building. It was time for their day to begin, and Julianne had some work to do in her room before the children started arriving.

"There's Betty," Maggie remarked as she watched their director getting out of her vehicle. "She had dinner last night with Warren again. That's the third evening this week they've been out together. Maybe Warren Sinclair would be a good man for Luke to meet. You know what I mean, Julianne? Warren lost his wife about a year ago, and he's been able to get on with his life."

Julianne sighed and walked through the heavy wooden door. Arguing this matter with Maggie was obviously hopeless until Maggie actually started listening, and Julianne had work to do before her classroom was invaded by four-year-olds.

A short time later, a light rap on Julianne's classroom door alerted her to the fact she'd neglected to open the door for the parents to enter.

"Miss Quinn?" It was Luke O'Hara's voice. Low

and quiet. Just like it had been on the phone last night.

Julianne pulled the door open the rest of the way. "Come on in, Mr. O'Hara. Good morning, kids. How are you today?"

"Okay," Nora and Todd answered almost simultaneously as they burst through the door and ran toward the play area in the rear of the classroom. "Let's get the animals out," Nora suggested, and Todd followed her lead.

"They've been up for over an hour," Luke remarked, watching his kids begin busily playing with toys they'd grown accustomed to in only one day. "They really seem to like it here." He looked from his active children to the young woman who had made them feel comfortable and accepted yesterday—enough so that they were anxious to return again today. So, this Julianne Quinn that his sister had bragged about might really be as good with children as Maggie claimed she was. She'd certainly worked wonders with his twins the first day. Maybe it was that soft voice, he considered. That same thought had occurred to him last night when they'd talked briefly on the phone. Julianne had a soothing manner in the way she spoke. It was something the children could respond to favorably. Who wouldn't? he wondered momentarily, then dismissed the thought. He had a busy schedule today. There wasn't enough extra time in his day to ponder the qualities that made Miss Quinn a good teacher. "I'll be back around four-thirty this afternoon," he stated matter-of-factly.

"All right, Mr. O'Hara. We'll look for you then," Julianne replied and smiled at the tall man who stayed near the door as he watched his kids play. His hair was combed casually to the side and slightly windblown, Julianne noticed. She had this unexplainable urge to reach up and smooth it back into place. The thought startled her, and she glanced nervously away from Luke. Maybe she'd been listening to too much of Maggie's rhetoric. "Enjoy your day, Mr. O'Hara," she added in a very businesslike tone. "Don't worry about your children. I'm sure they'll be fine here at the center."

Something had changed her mood abruptly, Luke was aware by the tone of her voice, but the cause of the change eluded him. Then again, women quite often were hard to understand as far as he was concerned. Kimberly certainly had been, and even his own sister was, at times. But he didn't want to think about that now. The work he had lined up with several branches of a bank in Minneapolis awaited him, so Luke thanked Miss Quinn for her help and turned to leave the room. He was halfway down the hallway before he missed that fragrant flower scent that had lightly hung in the air in Julianne's classroom. He recalled that Nora had remarked yesterday that her teacher "smelled good." Now that he thought about it, he realized he agreed with his daughter.

But that second day in Miss Quinn's classroom didn't go quite as well as the first for the O'Hara twins. Things seemed fine and all six of her children were busy and content until late in the afternoon when the skies outside turned stormy. They were in the activity room playing ball when a tornado siren unexpectedly sounded, upsetting all of the kids in Julianne's group. Especially Nora and Todd O'Hara. Julianne sent her teaching assistant down to Betty Anderson's office for help, and soon Betty was filling in for Maggie Wren with her group of newborns while Maggie hurried to her niece's and nephew's sides. It took the comfort of Aunt Maggie's hugs to stop their crying and settle them down enough to get through the remainder of that day.

Fortunately, Luke finished his work early due to the inclement weather and came to pick up the twins ahead of schedule. Nora, Todd and Julianne were all relieved to see him walk through the classroom door just as another clap of thunder crashed outside. The children ran into their father's arms with fresh tears and stories of the awful siren that had frightened them and how Aunt Maggie had come to "save" them.

Julianne gathered up Nora's and Todd's art projects they'd worked on in the morning and slid them carefully into the backpack they'd brought with them. Her assistant continued reading to the rest of the children, who were all seated in a circle, while Julianne spoke with the twins' father.

"I'm sorry, Mr. O'Hara," she offered quietly, frustrated and overly apologetic about not being able to console the twins by herself. She'd tried every way she knew to soothe their fears but had failed, and it discouraged her. She realized she'd underestimated the difficulties she might face with these two youngsters who had lost their mother. Her disappointment showed in the downward turn of her mouth, and Luke saw for the first time something other than confidence in the young teacher's expression. It looked a little like insecurity. Now, there was something he could identify with.

"Nora and Todd are fine, Miss Quinn. No harm done," he remarked while picking up his daughter, who had finally stopped crying. Todd's arms remained wrapped securely around one of his father's legs as Luke continued. "We can't...I mean, I don't expect things to go perfectly. Just do the best you can with them. That's all I've ever managed to do," he stated. "And Maggie's available when you need her. She's the reason we moved here."

Julianne caught her lower lip between her teeth and nodded her head, grateful for his understanding words. "I guess we should both thank God for Maggie."

But the straight line of Luke's mouth didn't give a fraction of an inch in either direction. "You'll have to thank Him for me, Miss Quinn."

"I will for now," she answered, remembering Maggie's mention of Luke's lost faith...and ignoring the warning that it was a subject better left alone. "And, maybe, someday, you can do so for yourself again, Mr. O'Hara."

Luke's blue eyes lit with what Julianne fully expected to be irritation. But if she'd have known him better, she'd have recognized it for what it was—simple surprise that this young woman, who couldn't be more than a few years out of college, would be so frank in her remarks to a man at least a decade older—a man in his position in life.

And just what was his "position in life," Luke suddenly wondered as he and the twins said goodbye to Julianne Quinn and made their exit from the center. He was...what? A father, the owner of his own business, a good provider for his family, a successful landscaper with excellent references, a widower. And, he had to admit, a man who only listened to his children's bedtime prayers instead of joining in.

That thought stung him as he lifted Todd into the extended cab of the truck. Nora scrambled in behind her sibling, and Luke helped them with their seat belts while his mind raced with discontent. Life had changed in so many ways this past year. But they were here, now, in Fairweather, Minnesota, close to his sister where he felt they belonged. This change was a good one, the right one. It had to be. He needed it to be.

Luke climbed into the pickup just as he noticed how dark the skies looked for so early in a summer evening. His wife had loved gray, dreary days. The cooler, the better. She said they reminded her of her childhood in New England, where she'd grown up. Home, she'd called it—regardless of the many years she'd lived in Chicago. That had bothered Luke. He'd wanted home to be where he was, where they were making a life for themselves, raising their children. He hadn't asked her to move to Chicago. She was already living there, managing several dress shops, when he first met her. So, why had her home-sickness for New England made him feel guilty? The answer to that question, he'd not found; but he'd taken some comfort in the fact that he'd arranged to have her buried there. At home. In the space next to her mother and father, both of whom had preceded her in death.

He started the truck and headed toward Olaf's Deli where he needed to buy milk and bread—necessities for breakfast in the O'Hara household.

"Daddy, can you get us some pickles?" Todd asked when his father pulled into a parking spot in front of the deli.

"Sure, son. C'mon," Luke answered, helping both kids out of the vehicle. "Let's go. Don't run."

The children ran through the front door toward the huge jar of whole pickles kept on top of the meat case. Luke bought several, together with the other items on his mental list. Maybe a scrap of paper and pencil would have been more reliable, but he hadn't taken the time to jot anything down. He rarely did. That also reminded him of Kimberly, almost as much as stormy days did. She'd been a chronic list maker, systematically marking off the numbered items as she completed them. All of that organization had disappeared from his life with her departure. And where had God been during all of that? Where was He *now*, Luke wondered.

"Can we eat the pickles now?" Todd was begging while Nora was busy reaching for the plastic bag that held their snack.

"Wait until we get home, you two," Luke answered. "You'll want drinks, too, and I don't have any in the truck. Come on, we'll be there in five minutes.''

The kids didn't seem to mind another night of frozen dinners in their small utilitarian kitchen filled with only the basic appliances. They ate their fish sticks, French fries and peas, and then rushed into the living room to watch a favorite cartoon while Luke cleared the table. It was when he was adding today's dirty silverware to yesterday's in the dishwasher that he suddenly noticed the mostly bare counters. The only homey touches were a basket of now wilting flowers that Frank and Maggie had sent and a large ceramic cookie jar with a comical cat painted on the front that Maggie had purchased, filled with homemade goodies and delivered on moving day. Luke had meant to buy some cookies from the bakery and replenish the supply, but he'd forgotten to do so. Maybe, tomorrow, he told himself. Maybe tomorrow, he'd get things right. But, deep in his aching heart, Luke knew his sister had been accurate. She'd warned him that nothing would be really right with him ever again, not until he made peace with the Lord he used to trust. Luke knew that would not happen until he could pray again...and he wasn't sure that day would ever come.

The next day went by quickly with Luke dropping off and picking up Nora and Todd at the center as he had done on previous days. The weather was very warm and another storm slowed Luke's landscaping work in the city that afternoon. But when the morning of the Fourth of July finally arrived, it promised to be a gorgeous day—just as Maggie Wren had hoped it would be. There wasn't a storm cloud in the sky. Julianne was up to see the sunrise that morning through her kitchen window, but only because she had promised Maggie she'd make a banana cream pie for their lunch. Otherwise, she would have slept in.

Dumping a small amount of flour on her counter, she soon finished her least favorite part of the job—rolling out the crust. She used her mother's recipe for a double crust so she filled two pie plates instead of one. The second one she was considering keeping for herself. Sometimes, at the end of a holiday, she'd come home to her empty apartment, make herself a cup of tea and eat something luscious as a reward for getting through the day without allowing herself to wallow in too much self-pity. The Fourth of July wouldn't be any different from the past few holidays she'd gone through without an engagement ring on her finger and Craig by her side. "But losing him was a blessing in disguise," she said aloud to the goldfish swimming in the bowl nearby. She really was thankful that the relationship was over; but Julianne missed the old feelings of belonging to someone, being half of a couple, believing in a happy, full future for herself.

The crusts went into the oven, 450 degrees for twelve minutes, and while they baked, Julianne went into the bathroom to apply her makeup. She had already showered and her shoulder-length hair had been styled into the slightly wavy look she normally wore. But it wasn't her clean skin or her blond hair that caught her attention in the bathroom mirror. It was the saddened expression she'd found looking back at her. One she'd seen too many times lately. One she was growing weary of.

Julianne hadn't realized how long she'd been standing in front of that mirror, just thinking, until the timer in the kitchen buzzed. She rushed to shut it off and retrieve the crusts from the oven.

"Today is going to be a good day, Goldie," she said to her tiny roommate. "No more moping around about being alone. I'm going to watch a parade, eat too much good food, and, in general, have a very fun day."

A couple of little bubbles rose to the top of Goldie's water, almost as if the fish were trying to respond to its owner's words. Julianne laughed. "Sorry, sweetie, but I don't speak your language," she said. Then she reached for some sugar and began stirring the pie filling. Soon she was slicing bananas and assembling her homemade creation to be shared with Maggie's family.

Julianne chose blue walking shorts and an appropriate white T-shirt with a design of blue-and-red fireworks brightening up its front and back. Loading her small wooden picnic basket with one pie and the packages of fresh hamburger buns she'd purchased at Maggie's request from Swenson's Bakery last night, she was ready to go. Julianne slipped her sunglasses into place, retied a running shoe that had come undone and, basket in hand, began the short walk to Maggie and Frank Wren's house. She knew

Luke and the twins would be there today. Maggie had made a point of telling her.

As Julianne neared her friend's home, she fretted about that disastrous experience with Nora, Todd and the tornado siren the other day. She certainly wasn't who or what they needed then, and she wondered how they would respond to her today. But when she rapped lightly against Maggie's screen door and then opened it to enter, she was instantly greeted with shrieks of joy from the O'Hara twins who ran to hug their teacher. "You're here! You're here!" Nora placed both hands on her hips. "We thought you'd never come," she scolded, which brought an immediate smile from Julianne.

"I had a pie to bake," Julianne explained and gave each child a soft touch to their cheek. "Where's your aunt Maggie?"

"She's in the kitchen, Julianne. She's getting ready to go to the parade with us."

"Thanks, kids. See you in a minute." Then she entered the homey kitchen of peach and soft greens. "So, I've progressed from Miss Quinn to Julianne?" she remarked to Maggie when she found her friend with her nose stuck inside the refrigerator. "I wonder how that happened?"

"Probably because they've heard me talking about you. I generally call you by your first name, you know," Maggie replied with a grin.

"And just what have you been saying? And to whom?" Julianne asked with a smile as she set her basket on the table. "Or need I ask?"

"Hello, Miss Quinn." Julianne turned at the sound

of the voice she recognized to see Luke O'Hara entering the room.

Maggie shrugged in answer to Julianne's abandoned question. "Oh, just some people, here and there. It's nothing to worry about. Luke, her first name is Julianne. And, Julianne, his first name is Luke. Try using them for a change."

Julianne laughed softly, nervously. "She's right, you know. We don't need to be so formal. How are you, Luke?"

"Fine, thank you. And you?"

Julianne nodded. "I'm okay. It's a beautiful day out there, isn't it? I mean, compared to yesterday...and the day before. You know, the rain, the tornado warning...the storm and all." Great, she thought. Let's see what other stupid thing I can ramble on about.

"Yes, it's good weather for the Fourth of July," Luke remarked. And he almost smiled. Julianne seemed off guard, maybe a little nervous; he couldn't decide exactly what was bothering her. But she definitely didn't seem quite as sure of herself as she usually appeared in the classroom.

"The parade starts in fifteen minutes," Frank announced as he walked into the kitchen with an armful of assorted flowers he'd gathered from the garden. He handed them to Maggie and gave her a light kiss on the cheek. "For you, my dear."

Maggie smiled. "Thank you, hon. They're beautiful." Then she reached into the cupboard under the sink for a large white vase. "I'll put these on the table."

Julianne's heart ached, mostly with jealousy, she supposed. She wanted what Maggie had. A man to bring her flowers, someone to kiss her with the assurance she was his to kiss, someone to love for a lifetime. She wanted to belong with someone the way Maggie belonged with Frank.

"C'mon, let's get going." Frank was giving orders instead of Maggie for a change. "Nora! Todd! It's time to go to the village green to watch a parade."

The children came running from the living room. "It's time?" Nora ran to Julianne while Todd grabbed his father around the leg.

"Yep, it's time," Luke answered, reaching down to pick up the little boy who looked so much like him. Then he glanced toward his daughter and her teacher. "Ready, Nora...Julianne?"

Both females nodded and Julianne smiled at the sound of Luke speaking her name. It sounded nice...so much better than "Miss Quinn." She took Nora's hand and they all started their walk toward the village green on that warm summer day.

The morning parade went as planned, and it delighted the twins. It was noisy, too long and handfuls of candy were thrown from many of the passing floats and vehicles. The fire engines from Fairweather and neighboring communities were part of the procession with their sirens blaring. The volume worried Julianne as she remembered the fiasco with the tornado siren. Todd seemed unaffected by it all. The noise, however, did send Nora into her father's arms with her ears covered but with a grin on her face.

The community came together after the parade for the afternoon festivities on the village green. The church picnic was attended by virtually everyone in Fairweather and many from Baylor's Landing. If the attendees themselves weren't official members of The Old First Church, they were either related to or friends with someone who was. The hours were filled with speeches from the mayor and Reverend Ben Hunter as well as patriotic musical selections performed by the Fairweather High School band. The contest for the Strawberry Queen was held and the pretty red-haired daughter of the local police chief was selected by the judges amid applause and cheers from the crowd. Emma Fulton, a former Strawberry Queen herself, had the honor of placing the golden tiara upon the reigning queen's head.

Concession stands practically covered the village green, and there were red, white and blue balloons and streamers everywhere. The strawberry shortcake stand, coordinated by Betty Anderson, offered more dessert than they could eat for two dollars with all of the proceeds going to the anticipated expense of the Harvest Celebration to be held in the fall.

Maggie and Frank, Julianne and Nora, and Luke and Todd spent most of the day together in a group, much to Maggie's dismay. She kept trying to shoo Julianne and Luke off by themselves—to eat strawberry shortcake, play a carnival game, listen to the local entertainment at the bandstand...anything without the kids tagging along. But it didn't happen that way. The kids were stuck to the adults like Velcro

all day. Not just to their father, whom they hadn't
seen enough of lately, but also to Julianne.

The affection Julianne freely offered was something the children seemed starved for, and the more
they needed from her, the more she wanted to give.
Julianne had been told by Maggie that she too often
thought of other people so much that she disregarded
her own wants and needs, but it wasn't going that
way with the twins. Nora and Todd's companionship
was exactly what Julianne needed and wanted that
beautiful Fourth of July. They turned that summer
holiday into the fun time Julianne had promised herself, and her goldfish, that she would have.

When time for supper came around, the Wrens,
the O'Haras and Miss Quinn returned to Frank and
Maggie's house where leftovers from the picnic became a light supper. The kids' excitement over the
impending fireworks display scheduled to take place
over Baylor Lake at night was wearing on Luke's
patience. He soon suggested they head over to the
lake where the kids could run and play for a while
until the fireworks started.

"Good idea," Maggie agreed as she patted her
plump tummy. "But this kid already has me worn
out," she said in gentle reference to the child within.
"I think I'll pass on the fireworks display this year.
But you and Julianne go ahead. The twins need to
get out for a while, and the lake would be a good
place to take them. Perhaps there will be other children there for them to play with." Frank went to
Maggie's side, slipping a hand around his wife's
waist.

"I'll stay here with Maggie," Frank said. "You okay, honey?"

Maggie nodded and smiled. "I think so. I'm just tired from today's activities. That's all."

Luke looked toward Julianne, who was playing cars on the floor with Todd and Nora. "Will you come with us?" he asked as he watched her race a small metal car up Nora's arm prompting a round of giggles from the child. Then Julianne looked up.

"Yes, Luke. I'd like that," she answered. Then she saw what she thought could be the hint of a smile at the corners of his mouth. After enjoying this day with him and his kids, getting him to smile was becoming almost a personal challenge.

They all thanked Maggie for her good food and hospitality that holiday. Then the four of them headed toward the truck. The kids climbed into their usual seats in the extended cab and then Julianne slid into the passenger seat. She knew she probably should feel nervous about going off like this for the first time with Luke; but with two rambunctious children in the back seat, she gave little thought to the matter.

The ride to Baylor Lake took only minutes since it was a short three miles from the center of Fairweather. The kids had barely finished singing some silly song when Luke pulled into a parking spot at the far end of the lake.

"Can we sit in the back of the truck while we watch the fireworks?" Todd asked.

Nora reached underneath the seat to pull out a

blanket. "No, Todd, because Aunt Maggie sent this blanket for us to sit on. Remember, Daddy?"

"No, I don't remember that, Nora, but it doesn't surprise me. Maggie seems to think of everything." Luke walked around the truck to open the door for Julianne.

"Aunt Maggie thinks of everything, and God takes care of everything," Todd said from his seat in the back of the vehicle. "Doesn't He, Daddy," Todd added matter-of-factly.

Julianne's eyes widened in surprise. Wasn't this the forbidden topic Maggie had warned her about? She looked from Todd straight into Luke's frowning face as he gripped her arm firmly enough to help her from the truck without responding to his son's statement.

"He didn't hear that from me, if that's what you're thinking," Luke remarked quietly and moved his hand away from Julianne's arm once she had her feet firmly on the ground.

Then Todd continued, "He takes care of me, He takes care of Dad and Nora and Julianne and the flowers and the lightning bugs—"

"Lightning bugs!" Nora interrupted when she jumped out of the truck. "Let's catch some!"

"Both of you stay where you can see me," Luke instructed his children. They ran through the grass in their shorts and bare feet with the carefree laughter it sometimes seemed to Luke only kids could have.

"Stay where they can see you instead of where you can see them. That's a good idea," Julianne commented. She watched Luke spread out the blanket Maggie had sent with them, and they sat down together. "It gives them clear boundaries."

"All they have to do is look for me. That keeps it simple," Luke said. "Julianne...I'm sorry if I was sharp with you a moment ago when Todd was talking about God. I didn't mean to be rude."

"You weren't," she replied. "Maggie mentioned to me that Christianity was a subject better left alone. For now, at least."

"For always would suit me just fine," Luke added, and glanced at the woman seated next to him on the ground. He hadn't been this alone with a woman since Kimberly. And he didn't feel too comfortable with the idea of being here, like this, with Julianne Quinn even now. No matter how great she was with his children or how pretty she was. Whew. Now, there was a thought he hadn't had before about Miss Quinn. Had he?

"Don't worry," Julianne assured him with gentle words. "I didn't come along to preach to you. I just came to see the fireworks."

Luke nodded. That's the only reason he was here, too. Wasn't it? "So..." he began with some awkwardness "were you here in Fairweather for last year's Fourth of July celebration?"

"Yes," Julianne answered. She'd been with Craig Johnson then, but there was no reason to point that out. Luke would probably start pondering what was wrong with her if he knew she'd been jilted by someone. Unless... She wasn't really sure what Maggie may have told Luke about her. Not that it really mattered. "I've been living in Fairweather and teaching at the center since I graduated from college three years ago. So, I've seen these local fireworks before. I guess I should warn you. They're not anything to get excited about.''

Luke motioned toward the children. ''As long as they enjoy the show, that's good enough for me.''

Julianne nodded in agreement and gave a soft laugh that Luke enjoyed hearing. He looked her way again and studied her profile as she watched the kids chasing bugs. Her features were beautiful. Not just pretty, but actually beautiful and with very little makeup as far as he could tell. She was what Maggie called a real heartland, natural-looking type. And Maggie had been accurate, although it had taken Luke until this moment to fully realize that fact. Tall, blond and brown-eyed, Julianne was nothing like his late wife, and yet she was every bit as lovely—all in her own way.

Julianne's eyes remained on the children while Luke's gaze lingered on her. She knew he was looking at her, really looking at her—maybe for the first time—and she wasn't ready to look back. Dusk was settling in, and the children were heading back toward their father and teacher. The twins ran up and plopped down on the blanket between them. ''Is it time yet?'' Nora asked.

''It won't be long,'' Julianne answered. Feeling the weight of Luke's gaze shift from her to his children, she relaxed considerably. She glanced over at him while Todd climbed into his father's lap. Luke's eyes were the same shade of blue as his shirt, and blue was Julianne's favorite color. In shirts and eyes.

The sun set quickly and soon the sky was filled with brilliantly colored displays of light. Streaks of gold impressed the children most, if their "oohs" and "aahs" were any indication. Red, white, blue, green and gold lit the sky over Baylor Lake as dozens of bystanders enjoyed the show. Some children nearby had sparklers with which they ran in circles, leaving a trail of smoke behind them. Nora and Todd wanted some sparklers of their own, but Luke refused. That would be a privilege they could have when they were older, but not now at age four. Amazingly, they accepted his words and settled back into watching fireworks exploding in the evening sky amid booms and crackling noises. Even Luke smiled that night, much to Julianne's amazement. The children's antics during the show brought laughter and smiles from both adults. Julianne was almost as sorry to see the holiday come to an end as the twins were, although she definitely wasn't reduced to tears by it as both of the kids were. She carried Nora and Luke picked up Todd, so they could get them back in the truck for the trip home. Julianne shook out the blanket they'd been sitting on and tossed it over the children once they were buckled into the back seat of the vehicle. Luke opened the door and helped Julianne into the truck. By the time they were out of the parking area, Nora and Todd were both sound asleep.

"They're exhausted," Julianne remarked.

Luke agreed. "They've had a very fun day. Mostly thanks to you."

"I enjoyed the day, too, Luke. Very much," Julianne admitted. "Mostly thanks to them." And their father may have had something to do with it, too, she thought, but did not say.

The ride to her apartment was short and quiet. Julianne directed Luke to the postmaster's large old house and pointed out her upstairs apartment.

"Thanks for the ride home," she offered and reached for the door handle to let herself out of the truck.

"I'll walk up there with you," Luke said. "That's a long, dark stairway to be climbing by yourself this late at night."

"No, don't." She reached across the seat and touched his arm, wanting to emphasize that she didn't need his assistance; but once she'd placed her hand against his warm arm, she regretted the action. It had been too personal, almost inappropriate, and she wasn't sure how to undo what she'd done except by pulling her hand away. Quickly. "I'm sorry, Luke, I just meant that I can go upstairs by myself. I've done that hundreds of times—alone. I'm not afraid. And, anyway," she added, nodding toward the sleeping twins in the back seat, "I wouldn't want you to leave them alone in this dark truck even for a few moments. If they woke up, they'd be frightened."

Luke agreed, although somewhat reluctantly. He thought the children would be fine sleeping right where he could see them from her stairway, and he certainly wasn't used to dropping a woman at the curb and letting her fend for herself to get inside her front door. This hadn't exactly been a date, he realized. He hadn't been on a "date" in over ten years, but he did feel responsible for seeing her home safely. Then he had an idea.

"Do me a favor, Julianne. Once you get inside and lock the door behind you, wave to me from that front window." Luke pointed up to where she'd left a light burning in the kitchen window. "That way I'll know you got in all right."

"Okay," she agreed, then opened her door and slipped easily out of the cab before he had the chance to help her. "Thanks for everything, Luke. I had a really good time today," she said with a heartfelt smile—the same warm smile Luke had seen from her during the fireworks display. It was one he liked seeing again.

"I enjoyed the day, too," he began, then paused. "Julianne, you're great with my kids."

"Thank you, but if I am, it's only because I'm a teacher."

But Luke disagreed. "No, it's something more than that," he stated. "They really had fun today. I think this is the best holiday they've had since...for the last year or so. Thank you."

"You're welcome," she answered, her smile fading. She should close the door to the truck and head up that stairway, she knew. There really was nothing left to talk about at this point. Except... "Maggie looked very tired when we left. Do you think she's okay?"

"I hope so. Frank mentioned to me the other day that he's worried about her getting too tired during her pregnancy. He thinks she's working too hard at the center.''

Julianne agreed. "She probably is. You know how Maggie is—she gives too much of herself to everything she does.''

"I know. She even wants to watch the kids for me tomorrow so I can go to Minneapolis and get caught up on my work. Being rained out again on Thursday put me behind schedule.''

Julianne's own giving-too-much-of-herself-to-everything trait kicked into gear. "I could watch them for you. That would allow Maggie to rest, and you could still get your work done,'' Julianne suggested. "I hadn't planned to do anything special tomorrow.'' The only activities she'd be giving up were cleaning the apartment and grocery shopping.

"But you work with my kids five days a week, Julianne. I can't ask you to keep them on your day off.''

Julianne looked toward the two children sleeping safely in the back of the truck. "You're not asking...I'm offering,'' she replied, then returned her gaze to Luke's uncertain expression.

Luke hesitated. He needed to work tomorrow to stay on schedule. And the kids did seem to be crazy about Julianne. "Are you sure it wouldn't be an imposition? I mean, you've just spent this entire holiday with them.''

"I really like Nora and Todd. I'd enjoy having them for another day. That is, if it would be okay with you.'' She tucked wispy blond hair behind an ear. Working at the center was one thing, but maybe

Luke O'Hara wouldn't trust her enough to leave his children with her alone, here at this tiny apartment with an ominous stairway for them to climb up...or to fall down. "I could take them over to the center, if you'd rather not leave them here—"

"No, here would be fine," Luke said. "But you'd need to be careful of the stairs. They'd both want to run up and down them." He glanced toward the black steps and railing.

Julianne smiled. She'd guessed his exact concern. "I will be. You don't have to worry."

"Better yet, why don't you watch them at my house? That way, they have their own toys and tapes, things to entertain them. And there's a fair-size yard out back for them to play in."

"That might be better. What time would you need me there?"

"Would seven o'clock be too early?"

"No, that would be fine. I'll see you then," Julianne answered.

Luke felt suddenly relieved. Maggie could rest, and the twins would still have someone they liked watching them. "Do you know where I live?"

"You bought the Taylor house on Spring Street, didn't you? Maggie mentioned it to me."

"Yes, that's the one. We'll see you at seven?"

"See you then. Good night." Julianne pushed the door shut and started for the stairway. She was up the steps and inside her apartment in a minute or less. Walking to the window that faced the street, she looked down to where Luke's dark blue truck was parked as he waited for her signal. She waved. She'd made it inside safely...that was, everything except her heart. Foolishly, she'd allowed it to become endangered in an attraction to this man whose own heart was broken, and Julianne knew no special cure for his kind of pain.

She watched Luke drive away and thought of Craig Johnson. Losing him had taken her a long time to get over, and that would be nothing compared to what Luke had lost. The woman he'd loved and chosen to spend his life with had been taken from him. He would need to heal slowly, from the inside out. It wasn't something anyone else could help him with. Only God could be his refuge now. If Luke wouldn't accept that, then the battle was his alone.

"But I can help him with his kids," Julianne said softly to herself. But, if she did, would she be setting herself up for more heartache? She groaned at the thought. Suddenly, that banana cream pie she'd saved for herself was starting to sound very good. Maybe she could drown her uncertainty in a slice. Or two.

Chapter Three

When the alarm sounded the next morning, Luke reached to shut it off quickly. Maybe the kids hadn't heard it ring. If they'd sleep in this morning, they'd be in a better mood for Julianne that day, and if he could make her day better in some way, he wanted to do it. Having Julianne in the children's lives was something for which Luke was beginning to feel very grateful. Even after only a few days, Nora and Todd seemed to have bonded with her in some very real, unexplainable way. But Luke wasn't looking for any explanations. He was just glad about this bit of good luck his family had happened upon and, although the old habit of thanking God had briefly crossed his mind, he chose not to. It seemed pointless to thank someone that, at times, you weren't even sure existed.

The holiday yesterday had actually been a pleasant one, much to Luke's surprise; the kids had been happy, content…not squabbling and wrangling with each other. Was it all because of Julianne Quinn? he wondered. It certainly seemed that way. He couldn't think of any other logical explanation.

Luke climbed out of bed and began to get ready for his day when it occurred to him that he hadn't dreamed of Kimberly last night. Not as far as he could recall. That had been the first time in over a year. Placing his razor on the edge of the bathroom sink, he stared into the mirror. Was that change because of Julianne, too? Luke couldn't answer that question, and he didn't know how to feel. Grateful or guilty? He'd loved his wife for such a long time. He loved her still. It was too soon, far too soon, the way he saw it, to notice another woman—no matter how easy she was to talk to or how good she was with the children. It just didn't feel right, and Luke was having trouble believing that it ever would.

The front porch light was on when Julianne pulled her small green car into a parking spot in front of the O'Hara home. The house was an attractive two-story home, an older style with white railing all around the front porch and a wide wooden swing for lazy summer evenings. The siding was yellow, quite cheery looking in the daylight; but this morning it was bathed in only streetlights and the front porch lamp. Julianne approached the wide front steps and hurried up them. She rapped lightly on the door, not wanting to wake the children if they were still sleeping. Almost immediately, Luke pushed the screen door open. He'd been watching for her. She stepped inside where the smell of coffee enveloped her.

"Hi," she said rather meekly. It seemed so strange, all of a sudden, being here in the early morning hours like this. She felt barely awake yet.

"Good morning. Want some coffee?" Luke asked.

Julianne smiled and placed her small canvas handbag on a nearby end table. "Yes, thank you. It smells good."

Luke directed her toward the kitchen and reached for a second clean cup from inside the dishwasher. "I don't like to empty this thing until I have to," he admitted. He closed the door on the appliance. "I never thought I'd be someone who'd even know how to operate a dishwasher, let alone the idea of loading and unloading one on a regular basis." He poured the coffee and handed it to the young woman who stood in his kitchen, a young woman about whom he really knew very little. So...why did he trust her as much as he did? "Cream or sugar?" he asked.

"Both," Julianne answered. "Drinking it black hasn't grown on me yet. I tried all through college to get used to it that way, but I never did."

Luke nodded toward the sugar bowl on the table. "And here's a spoon and saucer," he added as he pulled these items, too, from the dishwasher. Then he took a quart of milk from the refrigerator and placed it on the table. "Help yourself. I'm going to check on the twins. They were sleeping soundly when I came down here."

Julianne set to work on making her coffee palatable. She would have much preferred a cup of tea but wouldn't have dreamed of asking for it. Luke probably wouldn't have any tea bags in the house, anyway. He didn't look like the tea-drinking type.

She glanced around the kitchen. It seemed bare, so white and sterile looking. The lack of a woman's touch was quite evident everywhere. Empty counters, canisters that didn't match, the simple white blinds at the windows instead of curtains and the lack of pictures or drawings displayed on the refrigerator door—not even a magnet present with which a snapshot could be held. How odd, she thought. She was a single woman, without children, living alone yet she had more items stuck on the door of her refrigerator than this father of two kids had.

"They're still asleep." Luke's voice came unexpectedly from behind her. She nearly spilled her coffee.

"I'm sorry. I didn't mean to startle you," he apologized.

"You didn't. I mean, it's okay. Really." Julianne laughed lightly. "I guess I didn't hear you come back into the kitchen." She took a sip of her coffee. "So, do you want me to let them sleep until they wake up on their own? Or would you prefer I get them up at a specific time?"

"Never wake a sleeping child," Luke answered. "Never. That's always been my motto." He paused, suddenly feeling awkward about the situation. She was giving up an entire day to help him. And, why? "Julianne, are you sure you want to spend your Saturday this way? I can stay home today if you'd rather not—"

"I don't mind at all. Go," Julianne insisted with a determined look. "Get caught up on your work and don't worry about us. I'll have fun with the kids, Maggie will get to rest and you'll get some work done. We'll be fine."

Luke reached for his keys to the truck. "If you're sure…" He hesitated. "I can call to check on you around lunchtime. If you need me to come home then, I will."

"Okay," Julianne replied. "Would it be all right with you if I take the kids someplace? Maybe to Maggie's to check on her? Or to Swenson's for ice cream? Something like that?"

"Yes. I trust your judgment," he stated. And he did trust her for some undefinable reason. He looked from the ring of keys he held in his hand into Julianne's face, and he smiled a little. She looked sleepy. And young. Her blond hair was caught back in a ponytail and, at twenty-five, she seemed so fresh and alive. Luke wished he could feel that way again. Twenty-five felt like far more than ten years ago for him.

The silence between them made her uneasy. "Is there a number where I could reach you? Just in case I need to," Julianne asked before taking another sip of her coffee.

"It's on the table," Luke nodded toward a small yellow notepad. "I'll call around noon to see how it's going." He picked up the thermos and lunch he had packed for himself earlier that morning. He was ready to leave. Almost. "Julianne, thank you for doing this. It's not a small thing to give up your day off to watch Todd and Nora for me." He paused again. "I'll be glad to pay you whatever you—"

"You're very welcome and, no, I don't want any money," she stated firmly. "I'm doing this as much to help Maggie as to help you. Now, go. It's nearly seven-fifteen already. Didn't you want to be out of here by seven?"

"Okay," he turned to walk toward the front door. "Lock this door behind me."

"Yes, Luke," Julianne remarked. "I'm not exactly a fourteen-year-old baby-sitter, you know. Quit worrying. Just go."

Luke did exactly that. He quit worrying, got into his truck and headed for the city, leaving his kids in good hands. Julianne Quinn's hands.

Julianne and the children spent their Saturday doing a variety of things. First, there was the usual schedule of cartoons Nora and Todd watched while they ate their cereal and lay around in their pajamas on big pillows on the living room floor. There was playing ball in the backyard, fun in the wading pool, and then helping Julianne unload the dishwasher and find the right places to put the clean dishes away before reloading it with the dirty ones from the sink. Then they took a walk over to Aunt Maggie's which included a short visit with Uncle Frank at the Book-Stop, where they enjoyed a morning snack of crackers and juice.

"Thanks for watching the kids today, Julianne," Frank Wren said while he joined them in drinking a juice. "Maggie needs more rest."

"How is she feeling?" Julianne asked.

"Okay, I think," Frank replied. "But she's not one to complain much, so I'm really not sure. I'll be glad when she gets back in to see the doctor this week."

"Me, too," she agreed. "I promise we won't stay long, but do you think it's all right for me to take the kids over there to see her for a few minutes? Maybe five or ten?"

"I think she'd like that," came his answer. "She slept late this morning, so she's probably just eating her breakfast about now."

Frank was accurate, Julianne soon realized. When she and the kids arrived at the Wren home, Maggie was putting a slice of bread into the toaster.

Julianne kept her promise. They stayed less than ten minutes, long enough to satisfy Julianne's concern that her best friend was feeling better.

"I'm just tired," Maggie insisted. "The Fourth of July took too much out of me. The baby and I are fine, Julianne. Honestly. Don't worry so much."

After borrowing enough ingredients from Aunt Maggie to make snickerdoodles, the trio then walked back to the O'Hara house to bake the cookies, eat sandwiches Julianne had purchased from the deli for lunch and await Dad's phone call which came close to noon, just as he had said it would.

"Hello, Julianne? Is everything going okay?" Luke's voice sounded distant, almost as though he were in another state instead of a different city.

"We're fine, and we visited Maggie. She seems to

be doing okay, too,'' she assured him. "You want to say hi to your kids?''

"Sure. Put them on.''

Nora and Todd both spoke to their father, and stated emphatically they did not want him to come home yet. They wanted to play in the wading pool some more and eat the cookies they'd baked. They weren't finished with Julianne for the day, they claimed. Then Nora gave the phone back to their new favorite baby-sitter.

"They might not be finished with you, but are *you* finished with *them* yet?'' Luke asked with a laugh. "I can be home in half an hour, you know.''

"No, I'm fine, Luke. Honestly. Stay as long as you need to. We'll be here when you get home.''

It had been such a long time since anybody had said that to him. An unexpected stab of loneliness knifed through Luke's heart that hot summer Saturday in Minneapolis. He wanted a home again. Not just a house for him and the children to walk into at the end of every day, but a real home. One like Maggie and Frank had now; one something like he and Kimberly had known in their apartment in the city. A powerful wave of homesickness for someplace that didn't exist anymore swept over him, and he had to end the conversation quickly or Julianne would detect in his voice that something was wrong. So he gave a reasonable time that he'd return and said goodbye. Then he stood by the truck for a moment until he could regain his composure. He had a job to do; he had two kids to raise. He certainly didn't have time to stand around and lament all that he'd lost.

Life as he had known it was over. Gone. He thought he'd almost gotten used to that fact. Until Julianne reminded him of things better left forgotten.

It was late afternoon when Luke pulled up in front of the house. Both kids practically leaped off the porch, and they ran to greet their father with hugs and stories of the fun they'd had. Their excited chatter filled the air as Luke tried hard to listen to both of them at the same time.

"I can see you really missed old Dad today, huh?" Luke teased. He looked up from the twins' faces to see Julianne walking across the grass toward them.

"They did miss you," she offered. "They asked about you several times today, wondering what kind of trees Dad was planting and when you were coming home." Julianne crossed her arms in front of her as she spoke. Luke looked weary, she thought, or maybe he just seemed that way because his jeans and shirt were dirty from a hard day's work. Even with those observations, it struck Julianne how appealing this man could look, even at the end of a long day. His blue eyes were friendly with crinkly laugh lines at the corners which were actually visible today as he laughed with his children.

Julianne had enjoyed herself today. Too much. Why couldn't Nora and Todd have argued, back-talked, intentionally disobeyed her—anything other than having been the lovable, needy kids they were. A soft sigh escaped her. She'd done what she'd come here to do. It was time to leave.

"I think I'll go now, unless you'd like for me to

stay and watch the kids while you clean up,'' she began.

"Go?" Nora exclaimed. "But we're going out for pizza tonight. Please, stay, Julianne. It won't be as much fun without you!" The kids' protests continued until Luke interrupted.

"They're right, you know," he agreed with a steady gaze resting on Julianne's dark, gentle eyes. They were the prettiest brown he'd ever seen. "And after all you've done here today, you should at least let us take you out to dinner."

Julianne shook her head, but smiled. "Thank you, Luke, but you need time with your kids. You don't need me."

"Have they worn you out already?" he asked.

"No, it's not that," Julianne answered truthfully. Pizza with Luke and the children. Did she really want to move a step closer to them? And would eating a meal with them do that? Yes, she knew in her heart, it would do exactly that. "It's just that—"

"Come on, Julianne. Pleeease," the kids begged, cutting off her objections. "Come with us!"

"Maybe she has other plans," Luke remarked to the twins. She was young and pretty, he realized. She probably had a date with someone already scheduled for Saturday night. As a matter of fact, she could probably get a date with whomever she chose.

"No, I don't have plans," Julianne replied. Her stomach felt tied in knots, and it had nothing to do with hunger.

Luke watched her look away from him and guessed her nervousness. If they both were feeling awkward about this moment, maybe they should let it go. They could have pizza together some other day, maybe when they knew each other better. But then he glanced at the twins. "It will disappoint the kids if you don't join us," he remarked. "And I really don't want to spend the rest of the day with two crying children."

Julianne met his gaze again, this time with an understanding smile. "Looks like I'll have to go with you then. I don't want to ruin what's left of your Saturday."

"Good," Luke responded. "Would you mind watching the kids while I shower and change? It won't take long."

"Sure, that's fine," Julianne heard herself answer. How could she agree so easily to something so risky? How? She knew exactly how. By watching this man smile. It was a smile she had helped place there, and it could easily be her undoing. "C'mon, Nora, Todd. Let's pick up your toys in the backyard and get ready for dinner. Your father says we're going out."

The kids were shouting and running toward the back of the house to retrieve the toys they'd left out there by the wading pool with Julianne following along behind them slowly, thinking as she walked. Hadn't she asked the Lord to use her to help these children? Wasn't He doing so, here, today? Of course, He was. She was certain of it. And, if her usefulness happened to include dinner with two wonderful kids and their good-looking father, she'd have to endure it, she considered with a grin.

* * *

"Do you like pepperoni? Sausage? Mushrooms?" Luke asked as they glanced over the menus placed on the table of their booth for four.

"Yes, all of them," Julianne answered.

"We want cheese pizza, Daddy," Nora said. "Cheese, only. Like always."

"Why is it so dark in here? I want some lights on." Todd was squirming in his seat.

"The lights are always dim in here, son. You know that," Luke explained. "That's one of the reasons Nora likes this place."

Nora agreed. "It's neat! I like eating in the dark!"

Julianne laughed softly. "Actually, you're right, Nora. It is fun to eat by candlelight."

"A typically female response, I suppose," Luke remarked with a grin as the waitress appeared for their orders.

The pizza Luke and Julianne shared was hot and spicy, while the kids had their own individual cheese pizzas to enjoy, with soda and bread sticks.

Nora and Todd both tried their hand at some video games, but they mostly liked pushing the buttons without much understanding of how to actually play.

"I think four is a little young to comprehend the objective of this game," Julianne commented while reading one set of rules.

"But you're never too young to put quarters into a machine," Luke responded. "That's one of their favorite things to do."

"Then maybe we should let them put their coins into the jukebox. At least then we'd have some music to listen to in exchange for the expenditure of your money." She smiled. Julianne would be glad to have some control over the choice of songs being played. The last couple of tunes they'd been forced to listen to were love songs, and it made her feel very uncomfortable. More than that, she feared it might make Luke sad, and she didn't want to do that to him. So she and the children walked over to the jukebox to check out the selection. A couple of upbeat country songs seemed like the best option, along with a soft rock choice or two.

"I can't eat anymore." Nora finally admitted defeat some time later after trying to work her way through the four small pieces of pizza that made up her meal. "I ate too many bread sticks, Dad."

"That's okay. We'll take home the leftovers for tomorrow." Luke looked for their waitress in the crowd, and soon she came to their table with their check and a small cardboard box for the twins' leftovers. It wasn't long until they were back in the truck and on their way home. The kids fell asleep before they reached the house.

"They must have played hard today," Luke commented as he looked back at the children. He parked the truck beside the garage.

"They did," Julianne replied. "They should sleep well tonight." Better than she would, most likely, it occurred to her as Luke opened the door for her. She stepped from the vehicle to the ground, with his hand resting on her arm to steady her; then she moved past him quickly, away from his touch.

"If you unlock the front door, I'll carry them in

one at a time." He extended a hand, offering the keys to her.

Julianne took the keys from him and headed for the front door, which she opened easily. But then she went back to help. Luke already held Todd in his arms and was halfway to the house when Julianne offered, "I'll get Nora."

"She might be too heavy."

"No, she's not. I've picked her up before."

Julianne gently gathered up the limp form of the youngster in her arms, holding her close. She pushed Nora's bangs away from her sweaty forehead and placed a kiss there on her damp skin. Then she watched Nora's mouth curve into a smile even as she lay sleeping. A heaviness gripped Julianne's heart, bringing unexpected tears to her eyes as she held the little girl's warm body next to her. She blinked hard, not wanting Luke to see her reaction to the sad irony of the moment. A little girl, who needed a mother to love her, sleeping peacefully in the arms of a woman, who needed a child to love.

"Julianne?"

It was Luke's quiet voice behind her. She took a deep breath and turned to carry Nora into the house without meeting Luke's gaze. Maybe he wouldn't notice that emotion had made her eyes watery. But, by then, that same emotion had risen in her throat, threatening her with the fear of sobbing, right here, right now, and declaring how unfair life had been. To Nora and Todd. To Luke. To her.

"I'll take her," Luke offered and carefully took the child from her arms. He cupped Julianne's elbow

in one hand while balancing Nora with the other.
"C'mon," he tilted his head a little to the side toward the house. "Let's go in."

Julianne nodded, holding her lips tightly together,
afraid of the words that might come rushing out if
she let down her guard. Then she and Luke walked
upstairs to the twins' room where he placed Nora in
her bed, next to her stuffed rabbit. He leaned down
and kissed his daughter's forehead in exactly the
place she'd received a tender kiss moments earlier.
Julianne looked away and swallowed hard. She had
to get out of here, out of this house soon or she'd
make a complete fool of herself by crying over things
she couldn't explain. Then she felt Luke's hand
touch her shoulder, and she raised her tear-filled eyes
to meet his understanding gaze. He moved closer,
guiding her easily into his arms where she let go of
the sorrow as she buried her face against his chest
and wept.

How long they'd stood there, Julianne wasn't sure.
But when she was done crying, it was beginning to
get dark outside. She could see the colorful streaks
of fading sunset through the window of the kids'
room. Raising her head from where it had rested for
so long, she instantly missed the steady beating of
his heart against her ear.

Luke reached into a pocket to retrieve a handker-
chief and offered it to her. He cleared his throat
roughly before speaking. "I think that's supposed to
be the gentlemanly thing to do—offering your hand-
kerchief to a woman at a time like this."

At a time like this. What exactly was a time like

this? Julianne had just cried buckets all over a man whom she barely knew but with whom she almost felt she belonged. This made no sense. None, whatsoever.

"I'm sorry, Luke. I didn't mean to cry. I don't even...I don't even know you well enough to fall apart in front of you like that." Julianne's words were rambling, and she knew it. She was grateful when Luke raised a hand, touching his index finger to her lips, bringing an end to the talking.

"Julianne..." He started to speak, but stopped suddenly when her dark, earnest eyes met his. She'd never looked so fragile, so sad, so lovely. Luke stopped thinking. His hands moved to touch her face, and her soft skin felt warm against his fingers. Then his gaze slowly lowered to her mouth.

Julianne had to keep thinking. And clearly. She had to if she was going to keep herself from leaning forward into the kiss she suddenly found herself wanting.

"Julianne," he whispered her lovely name again in the stillness of the evening before his mouth brushed hers in a hesitant first kiss that did nothing to satisfy either's curiosity or longing. She instinctively followed his lead with a gentle response in an uncertain kiss, but when she raised her hands to place them lightly against his chest, some restraint Luke had been wrestling with, loosened. The next time his mouth touched hers, it was with certainty that she wanted this, too. His mouth moved firmly against Julianne's, both of them wanting something more of each other than they'd allowed themselves to admit

before now. And by the end of their kiss, Julianne
was afraid she could never get enough of this man.
Not if she spent the rest of her life trying. This was
not like any emotion she had known in her twenty-
five years. It was different. Deep. Endless, she feared.

They parted abruptly when Luke pulled away. His
head was down, his breathing ragged as he raised a
hand to his mouth. Then Julianne realized something.
This was most likely the first time he'd kissed a
woman since he'd lost his wife. Her heart ached for
him, for the conflict he must be feeling inside. And
for them...for what they could have together...if
they'd allow it to happen.

"I'm sorry, Julianne." Luke spoke first, quietly,
gently. "This probably wasn't the best time for
that."

She swallowed, choosing her words carefully.
"You don't need to apologize. I—I'm as responsible
as you are for, I mean, I wanted to kiss you, too."

Her statement drew Luke's attention back to her
face. She looked so beautiful. So vulnerable. And
there were so many things he needed her to understand. "It's not easy raising the kids alone, but I
don't want you to feel sorry for us, Julianne."

The strain in his voice surprised her. "Sorry for
you? Is that what you think this is all about? My
feeling sorry for you?"

Luke studied the disbelief in her brown eyes. He
hadn't meant to hurt her. But then he hadn't meant
to have these feelings for her—or to kiss her—either.
Why did he keep doing things he'd had no intention
of doing? "Maybe it's not me you feel sorry for,"

he continued. "Maybe it's the children. Maybe it's *all* of us. I don't know. Those emotions can get all mixed up inside and come out as something they're not."

"Not with me, they won't," Julianne insisted.

"I saw you with Nora...the sadness in your eyes," Luke remarked. "You want to fill that void in her life. You want to try to make things better for the kids, and you are doing that. In many ways." He shrugged his shoulders. "But you're so young. You'll find someone, have children of your own someday."

Julianne immediately lowered her gaze to the floor. He didn't know she could never have a child. Maggie must have kept the secret. She should have known her friend would, since she'd asked her to do so. But, Julianne feared, if she admitted the truth to Luke now, he would think she was drawn to him only because of the children. She didn't want that. "I asked the Lord to use me to help Nora and Todd when they first came to the center. I know you don't believe in things like that much anymore, Luke, but I do, and I think He is using me, here, with your kids. I don't know if we—you and I—fit into this picture yet or not. Time will tell, I guess. But as for the twins, I enjoy being with them. If I feel sorry for them, that's only part of my feelings for them. And for you," she added softly, hesitantly.

Luke rubbed a hand down his face and looked away from Julianne and all that youth and honesty and trust he saw. Trust in God, trust in him, trust in herself. She was too young and hopeful to be any other way. And he didn't want to take that away from her. "I can't give you what you deserve to have. Not now. Maybe never," he stated quietly. "It's too soon for me to think I can move on to another relationship." He looked back into her dark eyes now wide with question.

She nodded, noticing the tight, grim line of Luke's mouth. He was probably right. It might be too soon for him to have feelings for her, at least without guilt, she considered. He'd been happy once, and that had been taken from him. Who was she to think she could make Luke O'Hara happy again? She knew nothing about what he needed, what he wanted in life. The only thing she was sure of was that she was falling in love with his kids. Maybe this stirring of emotion she felt for him stemmed purely from her affection for the twins. Her feelings for Nora and Todd could be subconsciously pushing her heart in Luke's direction. Or maybe Maggie's encouragement had actually colored Julianne's thinking to the point of believing this could be a romance. And maybe, just maybe, Luke didn't feel anything at all for her. The kiss might have been meaningless to him. Maybe it was more of an experiment to see how it would feel to kiss another woman. Someone other than his wife.

"I should go," Julianne said and awkwardly hurried from the stillness of the children's bedroom down the flight of steps to where she'd left her purse on the end table.

"Julianne," Luke called after her, following her down the staircase. "Don't go."

"Actually, I think you're right, Luke," she said with more composure than she felt when she turned to face him at the foot of the staircase. She took a deep breath and exhaled. "We don't even know each other. The idea that we could have a romantic relationship may be ridiculous." There. She'd said what she needed to say to bring an end to this uncomfortable situation. "But if you're willing, I would still like to help with the kids. I don't think Maggie is able to help you much right now, with the baby coming. I promised Nora and Todd that I'd do some things with them, and I'll feel like I've been dishonest if I tell them now that I can't."

"Of course," Luke agreed. "I need all the help I can get with Nora and Todd." He raked a hand through his hair. "I guess that's obvious to you and probably the rest of the world, too."

She managed a small, tentative smile. "You're a good father, Luke. Don't be so hard on yourself."

His expression grew still and serious as he studied the unspoken hurt in her eyes. "I'm sorry, Julianne...."

But Julianne shook her head. "It's okay. When my engagement ended, I didn't think I'd ever be ready for another relationship. It took a lot of time before I agreed to go out with anyone else, and when I dated Reverend Ben—"

"Reverend Hunter?" Luke asked. He remembered meeting Maggie's pastor on moving day. He thought of the pastor and how suited to Julianne the man probably was. Looks, age, career. Luke didn't care much for the thought.

Julianne smiled. "We knew we weren't right for each other from the beginning, but a good friendship came from it. It was an important transitional time for me. I was finally ready to try again, when the time was right. Maybe that's what we're finding out about each other, too, Luke. If we can be friends, maybe you can move on from here to someday..." Find the right woman for you, Julianne had intended to add, but couldn't quite say the words. She tried again, "Someday you'll—"

"Kiss a woman without feeling guilty?" Luke asked, then gave a sad smile. "I doubt it." He was a widower, he realized. Free. Available. And he knew it as he stood looking at the lovely young woman who was about to walk out his front door. So, why did he still feel very much like a husband?

Julianne's mouth turned down in a moment of pure sorrow. She reached up instinctively, without thinking, and touched his face. Luke raised a warm hand to cover hers, pressing it against his cheek. "Good night," she said simply before pulling her hand away and walking through the front doorway toward her car.

"Call me when you get home," Luke said to her as she cut across the grass. "I want to know you got in safely."

Julianne agreed to do so, and then climbed into her car and shut the door. This was probably for the best, she told herself as she started the short drive home. She was too emotionally involved with Luke's children to think objectively about her feelings for him. Of course, she felt attracted to him. How could she not? Maggie expected it, Ben Hunter expected it...maybe even Julianne herself had expected it and made it happen. And Luke, he wasn't ready for another woman in his life. Not when Kimberly O'Hara still occupied his heart so completely.

She soon pulled into her usual parking space in front of the house and headed upstairs to her apartment. Maybe Luke was right. Maybe her feelings were all mixed up inside. How could she know how she felt about him when she was feeling too much, too fast?

Julianne picked up the phone to make the call. Luke answered on the first ring.

"Hi, I'm home. Everything's fine," she assured him.

"Good. Thanks for calling," he responded in the awkward exchange. "I...we'll see you Monday morning."

"Okay. Good night." She started to hang up.

"Julianne...thank you for today. And yesterday."

"You're welcome, Luke. See you Monday." Julianne wanted to put an end to the conversation. As she hung up the phone after his goodbye, it occurred to her that what she really wanted to end was the way she felt tonight. Stupid. Gullible. Easily swayed by other people's opinions.

She moved from the kitchen to her bed, sitting down on the edge of it. Then she pulled her feet up and lay down on the old quilt that covered her sheets. "Lord, I'm sorry I was so foolish," she whispered. "I wanted to help Nora and Todd. Now, I may have messed things up by—'' By, what? Kissing their father? Was that such a crime?

No, she knew it wasn't, but she also knew it might be enough to make the relationship strained from now on. "If You can get us past this stupid mistake, I'm still willing to spend extra time with the twins. They need a woman in their lives, and I don't think Maggie is physically able to help them much during her pregnancy. And You know how badly Frank and Maggie want this baby. Don't let her do anything that would endanger this pregnancy. If I can help out with the twins and keep Maggie from doing too much, show me how. And help me to accept the truth about Luke. He's a good man, a good father and I don't have to fall for him just because other people have put that thought in my head. Let me get past these silly romantic notions, and help this man with his kids. We could be good friends if we'd allow it..."

Julianne's prayer gradually came to an end, but she remained there awhile. Thinking. Being a friend to Luke, she considered. Was that possible? Raising a hand, Julianne touched her warm fingers to her lips. She'd never had a friend whom she hoped would kiss her. Again. Like that.

Chapter Four

Knocking on the door of the O'Hara home early the next morning wasn't easy for Julianne. If Maggie hadn't called and begged her to pick up the twins for Sunday school, she wouldn't have considered facing Luke again so soon. Not after yesterday.

"You owe me one, Maggie," Julianne mumbled under her breath as she knocked a second time. What if they weren't up yet? What if Maggie was wrong, and they weren't expecting her? What if she was actually waking up the whole family this early on a Sunday morning?

Just then, the door flew open.

"Julianne! Aunt Maggie promised you'd come!" Nora rushed into her teacher's arms. "See, Todd, I told you!" she called back to her brother who came running toward them for a hug of his own.

"Good morning, kids." Julianne's needless nervousness disappeared at first sight of the children. "Ready for Sunday school?"

"Yes, we're all ready," Nora said and looked down at her blue-and-green striped sundress. "See my dress?" She turned around in a full circle, several times, to show off her outfit.

"Yes," Julianne answered with a soft laugh. She touched Nora's beaming face. "It's beautiful."

Just then, Luke appeared at the door and picked up his young model. "Did you tell Julianne who ironed that dress this morning so it would look so pretty?" His grin was broad as he looked toward Julianne. "It's nice of you to pick them up this morning, but I asked Maggie not to bother you. After spending the last two days with us, I thought you deserved a break."

"I don't mind, Luke. I'm going to church, anyway. I may as well take Nora and Todd with me. Are they ready?" She turned her attention away from his unshaven face to the children. He'd look good with a beard, she couldn't help thinking. Right, Julianne, she chided herself. And you're just going to be his friend? "Come on, kids. Let's go. I've got a Sunday school class to teach."

Luke opened the door for them, and they all stepped out onto the porch. "Be good," he ordered and kissed both kids on the top of their heads before they jumped off the porch and ran toward the car parked in their driveway.

"You teach a four-year-old class at church, too? Is there no end to your masochistic tendencies?" he asked.

"No, actually I teach third and fourth graders. They have a slightly longer attention span," she answered and stepped off the porch. "And, sometimes, only slightly."

Luke's laugh was quiet. "I know what you mean." Then he nodded toward his children. "If they don't behave, tell them no dessert today."

"And that will take care of it?" she asked in a voice filled with skepticism.

"It might. A neighbor brought over a plate of homemade chocolate chip cookies yesterday evening. Nora and Todd got into them this morning, so I had to hide them in the cupboard. They won't want to lose the privilege of eating some later."

Julianne raised her hand to protect her eyes from the early-morning sun as she glanced across the street in the direction of the neighbor's house Luke had nodded toward. Holly Nelson's home. She was a divorced mother of two and an elementary school teacher who was apparently interested enough in Luke O'Hara to deliver baked goods to his front door. A streak of jealousy like she'd never felt before shot through Julianne. Not even when she'd caught Craig Johnson openly flirting with a classmate in college did she feel as instantly angry as she did in this moment. And it was foolish. Childish, even. She had to change this way of thinking before it ruined whatever relationship she could have with Nora and Todd. Those children needed some tender loving care, not plates full of sweets.

"I'll have them home by noon," Julianne told him before walking away. Chocolate chip cookies. How very unoriginal, she thought after Luke thanked her and they went their separate ways. Surely, Holly Nelson could come up with a better idea than that. Like what, Julianne could almost hear Holly ask. Taking his children to Sunday school?

The morning at church flew by for Julianne. After leaving the twins in their Sunday school class, she went to teach her own group of children. Then during the morning service, both Nora and Todd lost their dessert privileges for various offenses before it was time for children's church; however, Julianne gave them ample opportunity to earn them back again before she took them home to their father for the rest of the day.

Declining Luke's offer of lunch, Julianne went home to spend the remainder of her Sunday trying to get caught up on some of the things she'd neglected over the past few days. But being in the quiet apartment with no one but the goldfish didn't feel quite right today. She missed Nora and Todd. Tomorrow morning she would see them, and the next day, and the next, she knew; but seeing them at the center and being with them at home were two entirely different feelings. Their laughter, their silliness, the warm hugs they were anxious to give and receive, she missed all of it. They were needy little souls. She'd known that instinctively the first moment they met. What she hadn't expected was the discovery of how needy her own heart was.

The longing for children of her own had been pushed to the back of her mind for so long, she thought she'd almost come to grips with the knowledge she'd never have any. But Nora and Todd brought a rush of emotions to the surface that Julianne wasn't prepared to deal with. She would need God's help to sort out all of these feelings and figure out what to do with them.

"'Commit thy way unto the Lord; trust also in Him; and He shall bring it to pass.' Psalm 37:5," she repeated from memory. "I do trust You, Lord," she said, "I trust You to show me what I'm supposed to do here. Nora and Todd are wonderful kids. Helping their father is something I'm willing to do, but at what cost to myself? A broken heart someday when Luke no longer needs my help with the two children I've fallen in love with?" Did the Lord want her to open her heart up to that possibility? And would the tender smiles of those two motherless children allow her to do anything less?

Monday morning brought cloudy skies and the threat of rain convinced Julianne to drive to the center rather than walk. She thought she'd be the first one there that day, but Maggie had already unlocked the front doors and turned on the coffeepot in Emma Fulton's office by the time Julianne entered the building.

"Good morning! How are you today?" Maggie greeted her friend with a warm hug.

"I'm fine. How are you? And what are you doing here when you should be home resting? We can find a sub to work with the babies today," Julianne said. "Let me check with Betty—"

"No, no, no. I'm fine this morning. Honestly." Maggie raised a hand as if swearing to the truth. "If

I felt bad enough to stay home, I would have. Now, Frank has been nagging at me plenty, so I really don't need to hear it from you, too." She reached for a plate from Emma's nearby desk. "Have a brownie. I made them yesterday, but they're still fresh."

"But you were too tired to go to church yesterday. How did you find the energy to bake?" Julianne asked as she sampled one of Maggie's treats.

"I felt much better in the evening. How did church go yesterday? Did you and Luke go out to lunch afterward?"

"No. He asked, but I couldn't go. I had to get some things done at home, Maggie."

"You turned down lunch with my handsome brother to stay home alone? With a goldfish? Have you lost your mind?" Maggie asked and reached for a second brownie.

"Not my mind, Maggie. My heart," Julianne said quietly and sat down on the corner of Emma's unoccupied desk. "I'm afraid I'm going to lose it completely."

"To Luke?"

Julianne shrugged. "Maybe, Luke. Definitely, the kids. I'm crazy about them. I want to take them home with me. Permanently. And I can't. It's not like they're up for adoption, you know."

"True," Maggie remarked. "Frank and I wanted to adopt them after Kimberly died, but Luke wouldn't consider it. They're his kids, and he didn't think he could go on without them. But don't you see? With Luke you could have it all. A husband, a ready-made family…it could be just what you need in this life, Julianne. Give it a chance.''

"It won't go anywhere. Luke can't think beyond his life with Kimberly. He's not open to anything else. I doubt that he ever will be,'' Julianne said, remembering their short-lived romantic moment.

"Well, that's quite a life sentence to label him with. Just because he's still grieving, doesn't mean he won't ever come out of it and notice what an incredibly beautiful, talented, brilliant—'' Maggie looked Julianne over from her blond head to her brown leather sandals ''—and shapely young woman you are. He's a man, Julianne. Give him some time to get used to being around you. Sooner or later, he'll realize how irresistible you truly are.''

"Yeah, right," Julianne remarked in a dull voice. "Just like Craig Johnson did." She reached for a cup and a tea bag from one side of Emma's desk. "I'm going to have my tea and go on to class. I've got some things to do before the children get here.''

"Craig Johnson was a self-centered jerk. He's gone and good riddance, that's how I've always felt about his departure from your life. It was a blessing from God." Maggie reached out to touch her friend's arm. "Luke needs you, Julianne. Don't give up on him because he's a little thickheaded right now. He'll come to his senses eventually. He's only been alone for a year, you know. It might take a little time.''

"For Luke O'Hara, it might take a lot of time," Julianne emphasized. She stood up to leave the room.

"Do you remember how despondent you were when Craig broke off your engagement? You weren't interested in anyone. Not anyone," Maggie reminded. "No matter how good-looking he was, what a great guy he was, if he was a churchgoer or not...nothing mattered to you but protecting that broken heart of yours. Do you remember those days?"

"How could I forget? They weren't that long ago," Julianne acknowledged.

"Exactly!" Maggie exclaimed. "It finally took Emma Fulton fixing you up with Reverend Hunter to snap you out of that zombielike state you'd been dwelling in. Remember how worried you were about going out with Ben? You were a real pain back then, I don't mind telling you."

"And? Your point is?" She would have loved to bring a quick end to their discussion, but knowing Maggie as she did, it wasn't likely.

"Luke is no different than you were. He's sad, Julianne. And he's lonely and probably a little frightened of taking any risks. Being attracted to you would be exactly that, you know. A risk."

Julianne didn't reply immediately. She had heard Maggie's words, the truth they held. The only problem was, she didn't want to help Luke in the way Reverend Ben had helped her. Ben was a friend; he would never be more. Deep in her heart, she wasn't sure she could play that role in the life of Luke O'Hara. "Maggie, I don't understand exactly what's happening with me right now. I barely know your brother, and, yet, I feel like...like I've always known him. I like the way he laughs, talks, smiles...and I have this wonderful rapport with his children. I even like that old house he bought. It feels so homey, so lived in. It reminds me of the home I grew up in.''

"So, just keep doing what you're doing, Julianne. Spend time with the kids. It's good for them and it helps Luke out immensely," Maggie encouraged, ''and my doctor did tell me I'm going to have to slow down until the baby is born, so I won't be able to do as much for Luke or the twins as I thought I would when they first agreed to move here. Just hang in there for now. If it's meant to be, it will work out. If not, you'll still have fun with the kids until my baby comes. Then I'll be more physically able to be the aunt they need in their lives.''

Julianne stared into the kind face of her friend. ''I know you mean well, Maggie, but—''

"Do this for me. If you won't do it for Luke or the kids, will you do it for me? Help them out a little until I can help them out more?'' Maggie pleaded.

"I guess I could.'' Julianne gave in. ''I've already told Luke I wanted to do some things with the children that I'd promised them, anyway.''

"Like shopping for new clothes?'' Maggie asked.

"Yes, how did you know?''

"Nora told me about some of your plans. Tuesday evening would be perfect for shopping. The kids are desperate for some good church clothes. And Friday night Frank and I are having pizza at our house with the twins since Luke has some work to do. I've already told the kids you'll be there. Frank has a couple of new family videos he's thinking of selling at the Book-Stop and he wants us to watch them first to see what we think.''

Julianne shook her head but smiled. "Anything else on my agenda I should know about?"

"Church next Sunday with the twins, if you wouldn't mind. I might not be able to go."

"You seem pretty healthy to me, Maggie," Julianne remarked with a mischievous lift of her eyebrows.

"But by the weekend, well, you never know how it's going to be with an old pregnant woman like me. I could be awfully tired by Sunday morning. The children enjoy being with you so much, anyway, I just thought it would be good for you to take them. If you or I don't pick up the kids, they don't go. Well, we just can't have that."

"Okay, Maggie, but I have to go to class now to get ready for the day." As she turned and started out the door toward the hallway that would lead to her classroom, Julianne added, "If you think of any other things I'm supposed to do, just type up a list and give it to me. Oh, and, Maggie, you might mention to your brother that most of these ideas are yours and that I'm not relentlessly pursuing him. These plans are less subtle than Holly Nelson's plate of chocolate chip cookies."

"Chocolate chip cookies? What are you talking about, dear?"

"Ask Luke," she answered, giving a soft laugh as she walked away. Nora and Todd she adored, yes. But Luke? What would he think of her increased involvement in his life? She was sure she'd find out. Eventually.

* * *

Julianne did take the children shopping Tuesday night as Maggie had arranged. They also went to a fast-food restaurant for dinner and a children's movie, giving their father an evening to himself. When she met the kids at Frank and Maggie's house Friday night for pizza, she was surprised to find Luke there, too. The evening was pleasant, the twins had fun and if Luke was bothered in the least by Julianne's continued presence in their lives, he certainly didn't show it.

After taking her home late on Friday, he asked if she could go with them to the zoo on Sunday afternoon. She said she'd go if she could take the children to church and Sunday school first, and he agreed. So picking up the twins on Sunday mornings became a regular routine for Julianne, and one she enjoyed.

Spending her days with Nora and Todd at the center didn't detract at all from the fun she had with them during many evenings of the next few weeks. The children were lively and bright, mischievous but desperate to please, and starved for affection. Julianne Quinn fell completely, hopelessly, deeply in love with the O'Hara twins. If she could have claimed them as her own, she would have in a heartbeat. They were everything she knew she'd never have in a life without motherhood—and that was the road she was facing.

Chapter Five

Luke grabbed the alarm clock, wanting to put an end to the noise that had awakened him when he noticed the numbers on the lighted dial—2:14 a.m. And the sound that had roused him was not that of the alarm, but rather the cries of Nora in the next room. His feet hit the floor, and he headed directly for his crying little girl.

"What is it, honey?" he asked quietly as he flipped on the teddy bear lamp on the twins' dresser. "Another bad dream?"

"I don't feeell good," the child wailed. "I want Julianne."

"Julianne?" he mumbled. Her request shouldn't have surprised him as much as it did. He'd known the kids had taken to Julianne with unusual enthusiasm right from the beginning, and with as much time as she'd been spending with the O'Haras—all three of them—Luke should have realized how attached to Julianne the children were becoming. It would have been enough to even make him a little jealous, if he hadn't welcomed the needed help Julianne provided. But, up until this moment, neither of the twins had ever asked for her to comfort them from an injury or illness. That had been his job, or Maggie's on occasion, for the past year. As Luke bent to scoop Nora into his arms, the feverish skin of her small body startled him, awakening him completely, instantly in a near panic. He held her close, and she buried her face in her daddy's shoulder, crying incessantly as he carried her into the bathroom to find the thermometer. Slipping it under her arm against protest, he held her tiny arm down as seconds dragged by. Why hadn't he taken the time to buy the new thermometer Maggie had asked him to pick up at the drug store last month—the kind that registers temperature through a child's ear within seconds?

Maggie, he thought. That's who he'd normally call at a time like this, but not tonight. Not with Maggie feeling so sickly herself now in the middle of her pregnancy. He couldn't disturb her with his troubles. But Julianne was a possibility. Calling her in the middle of the night like this was certainly asking a lot of her, but knowing Julianne the way he did, he didn't think she would mind the interruption to her night's sleep. In fact, Luke considered, she probably wouldn't like it if she knew Nora asked for her and he didn't call.

"Julianne," Nora said between sobs. "I want Julianne."

Luke pulled the thermometer from under his

daughter's arm after less than a minute only to see the mercury had already risen above 103 degrees. "Julianne," he said aloud to himself as he left the bathroom with Nora still crying in his arms, to head for the kitchen. Her phone number was scribbled on a piece of paper and taped on the wall next to the phone along with other important numbers such as Maggie's home, the day-care center and the tree nursery where Luke ordered many of the plants and saplings he used in his landscaping jobs. He punched in the seven numbers and hoped she'd be home.

"Of course, she'll be home," he said more to himself than to Nora. "Where else would she be at two in the morning?" Suddenly, he realized he didn't like the thought that she'd have other possibilities.

But she answered quickly. "Hello? Who is this?" Julianne asked in a groggy voice.

"It's Luke, and I'm sorry to call you so late."

Julianne's heart lurched in her chest. It must be something about Maggie...something horrible. After all, it was the middle of the night. "What's happened? Is Maggie all right?"

"Yes, she's okay. I'm not calling about her. It's Nora—" Then the wailing of the four-year-old drowned out her father's voice momentarily.

"Why is she crying?" Julianne asked, pushing some hair from her eyes as she listened to the sound. "Is she sick?"

"Very," Luke answered as soon as he could be heard again. "Her fever is a little over 103. I'm taking her to the emergency room just as soon as I can get Todd awake and both of them into the truck."

He paused. "She's asked for you. Repeatedly. Could you...would you mind if I stopped by and picked you up on the way to the—" Nora's crying drowned out her father's words once again.

"Get the kids ready, and I'll meet you at your house. That will save time." She hung up the phone and reached toward the dresser on which she'd left the skirt and sweater she'd worn to work that day. Then it occurred to her she hadn't given Luke time to agree or disagree. She'd basically just given orders. Not that it mattered much at this point, she thought as she hurried into the bathroom. Reaching for a brush, she pulled her long blond hair up into a ponytail. Shoes, she thought. Where had she kicked off her flats? In the bedroom? No, she didn't think so. She rushed into the living room of her small apartment and found them exactly where she'd left them—about six inches inside the front door. Slipping into the shoes, she opened the door and was about to step out into the light offered by her porch lamp when another small necessity came to mind. Keys. But they were easy to find because she always left them in the same place. On the key rack inside the kitchen door.

Within minutes she was driving across town toward the older two-story home that was spacious and had a lived-in look about it that she liked very much. Kind of like the people who had moved into it, she thought and then reconsidered. No, they meant much more to her than any house ever could.

Julianne pulled in front of the house and parked underneath the young maple trees that lined the front sidewalk. Lights from inside the dwelling along with the outside lights Luke had turned on for her, lit the yard. The red and pink impatiens that had been planted around the porch were lovely if Julianne had taken the time to notice, but she ran to the front door and turned the knob, sensing that Luke might have left it open for her. And she was right. She stepped inside.

"Luke?" she called out to him when she entered the house she'd become familiar with over the past few weeks. "Luke?"

Nora's crying had persisted throughout the short period of time it had taken Julianne to reach their home, and Luke was never more grateful to hear someone calling out his name as Julianne was now downstairs doing.

"C'mon, Nora, honey. Let's go," he said to the restless child in his arms. By the time Luke had walked out of the bedroom to the top of the staircase, Julianne was halfway up the steps.

"Nora? Sweetheart? Are you okay?" she asked.

Nora raised her head from her father's tear-stained T-shirt and extended her little arms toward her teacher. "Julianne! I knew you'd come," she exclaimed with a hiccup before sliding effortlessly into the comfort of Julianne's arms.

"Oh, honey...you feel so hot," she remarked and looked up at Luke, who had turned to reenter the twins' room. "Is Todd ready to go?" she asked while soothing Nora's damp forehead with a loving touch. "I'll take Nora out to the truck."

"Yes, he's ready," Luke replied and glanced

down at his own jeans and old work T-shirt. He guessed that would have to do. He didn't want to take time to change. Within a few minutes, Luke had gathered up a sleepy Todd, his wallet, checkbook and both kids' favorite stuffed animal, Nora's rabbit and Todd's basset hound puppy. Julianne reached out to take the toys from him once he reached the pickup in the driveway. Todd and Nora were both buckled into the extended cab—Nora under great protest while Todd couldn't have cared less. Julianne climbed into the back with Nora, tucking an arm around her.

"You're going to sit back there?" Luke remarked. He slid the keys into the ignition, and they started on their way.

"It will make Nora happier if I do," Julianne acknowledged, and she was right. Within minutes of pulling away from the curb, Nora and Todd were both asleep, although Nora's rest was fitful due to her high fever.

"Thank you for coming," Luke offered in a voice filled with obvious gratitude. "She started to settle down as soon as she saw you."

Julianne's mouth curved into one of those appealing smiles. He caught just a glimpse of it from the rearview mirror.

"I'm glad to help out," she commented. "I noticed Nora pulling at her ear while I was buckling her in. My guess is she has an ear infection."

"You're probably right. She's had them several times. Her pediatrician back in Chicago suggested having tubes put into her ears at some point if the problems continue.''

''Did you give her anything? For the fever, I mean?'' Julianne asked. ''You do know not to give her aspirin, don't you?''

Luke nodded and smiled. ''Yes, Maggie filled me in on a lot of life's little details after...'' he said, then paused. ''Once I was on my own with the kids.''

Julianne leaned over and kissed the mass of brown curls on the crown of Nora's head. She couldn't help but think of how much Luke and the twins had lost when Kimberly O'Hara died. Her own struggles in life seemed trivial in comparison. But the ride to the hospital would be long, and Luke was worried enough about Nora's fever. He didn't need any more distractions than that right now, so she changed the subject. ''At least it's the weekend,'' she remarked. ''I don't need to find a sub for my class at the center this morning.''

''I didn't even think of that,'' Luke responded. ''I should apologize to you for not considering how this might affect your schedule.''

''I'd have been hurt if you hadn't called me. There's no need to apologize. When you're a parent with a sick child, all you can think about is how to help your child.'' Julianne soothed Nora's damp hair from her forehead. ''I really think she'll be fine. Her fever is high but it's not unreasonable. With an ear infection, her temperature could easily be 103 degrees or more. Please don't panic until you know what you're dealing with.''

''Having you along helps a lot.'' Luke's spontaneous remark caught both of them off guard. He really hadn't intended to say that just yet.

"Thank you," she answered softly. "I'm pleased that Nora likes me enough to ask for me in a situation like this."

"Nora loves you," he responded. He glanced into the rearview mirror and caught Julianne's eyes. "Todd does, too."

The feelings were mutual, despite Reverend Ben's warnings of caution. Julianne was completely in love with Luke's kids, although she couldn't quite find the words to tell him just then. So she nodded her head.

The trip to the city took nearly half an hour, and in their concern for Nora's health, neither Luke nor Julianne had much else to say. Julianne was silently praying for the little girl and for Luke, that he would handle this matter calmly.

Prayers were not what was on Luke's mind that night. He was quiet, withdrawn. Thinking. About countless rides to and from another hospital during Kimberly's illness. He wanted Nora well and home as soon as possible. Hospitals were no longer easy for him to tolerate.

"There it is," Luke pointed out when he approached the facility. "Just up the road to the right. I passed it the other day when I was out here on a job. The emergency room is at the far end."

Within minutes, Luke was pulling up in front of the entrance. He pulled an insurance card from his wallet and handed it to Julianne. "You'll need this. Take Nora in. I'll park and bring Todd with me in a couple of minutes." He opened the door and helped Julianne from the truck and then placed a sleeping Nora into her arms. Julianne hurried into the hospital.

Luke glanced her way as he drove off toward the parking lot. A gush of air caught Julianne's ponytail and blew blond hair around her when the automatic doors swung open to grant her entrance. *Thank You for Julianne's help.* The words crossed Luke's mind but not his heart. He wasn't going to be thankful to God. Not yet. He wasn't even certain Nora would be all right. In fact, there were too many things in his life he wasn't certain of yet. And one was a decent parking place in this dark but crowded lot.

"Yes, here it is," Julianne said and handed the plastic insurance card to the receptionist who requested it. She was grateful Luke had thought to give the card to her since it was one of the first things the hospital staff asked for. "Yes, Nora O'Hara, *N-O-R-A.* She's four." Information was typed into a computer as Julianne sat, holding the whimpering, restless child on her lap in a small cubicle at one end of the emergency room. She was doing her best answering those questions she could, while watching the front entrance for a glimpse of Luke and Todd. "No, I'm sorry, I don't...I can't remember her middle name," she stated. She should have known it. She'd seen it on Nora's file at the center. Why couldn't she recall something so simple? And the puzzled look on the face of the gray-haired receptionist seemed to require an explanation. "I'm her teacher, not her mother. I'm here to help her father.

There he is now." Finally, after what had seemed like forever, they appeared. Luke was carrying Todd as he stepped inside and his eyes scanned the waiting area for Julianne and his daughter.

"Luke, we're over here." Julianne stood up and called out to him, motioning him to her side. "There are questions I can't answer. Why don't you take Nora and I'll go sit in the waiting area with Todd."

"No! Julianne, don't go," Nora pleaded.

Julianne leaned forward and placed a hand tenderly against the little girl's hot forehead. "I won't go far away. I promise. I'll be right over there with Todd, and if you need me, your father can find me. Okay, sweetie?"

Nora was crying softly. She nodded her little head before burying her face in her father's chest as Luke eased her from Julianne's arms into his own. Then Julianne was in charge of a sleepy Todd, who was struggling to keep his eyes open to see what was going on with his sister.

"Hold me," he stated more than asked, and Julianne scooped him up in her arms. Finding a seat nearby, she sat down and shifted Todd into the most comfortable position they could manage. Soon, he was asleep. The gentle rhythm of his breathing had a calming effect on Julianne as she listened to him. Thankfully, his forehead felt cool. Having one sick child at a time was more than enough to handle, Julianne felt certain, although she'd had little actual experience with situations like this. When any of her four-year-old students were sick enough to need a doctor, then they were sick enough to stay home rather than come to the center.

Caring for an extremely ill child wasn't something Julianne had dealt with before now; and from the tense look on Luke's face, this was something he apparently didn't know much about either. What a fine pair they were. Two people—in the middle of the night, in the heart of a hospital—frantic with worry over something that might very well be nothing to panic about at all. She sighed and brushed some brown hair away from Todd's closed eyes. He smelled of soap from his nightly bath, and Julianne inhaled the sweet scent.

Todd was usually such a busy little guy, exploring everything within his reach, and always with a smile or a giggle. At the end of the school day, after Luke picked up the kids, Todd's laugh was usually the first sound Julianne missed in the silence of her empty classroom. Working all day with children generally left her grateful when the end of the day arrived. But with Nora and Todd, things were different. She was only glad to see four-thirty come around if she was going to see them again that evening.

"Julianne." It was Luke's voice and she turned her head to see him walking toward her. "We're going back to an examining room now. The nurse just took her temperature and her fever has gone up another half a degree."

A wave of concern washed over Julianne. But a steady calm was what Luke needed from her now, not more anxiousness. "She'll be okay, Luke. The doctor will know what to do. Take as long as you need. Todd and I are fine here." Then she felt strongly prompted to say something more, maybe for Luke's benefit as much as for Nora's. "I'll be praying for her."

The tense lines on Luke's face relaxed a bit. Or did she just imagine it? She couldn't be sure. He nodded without responding and turned to follow a nurse down the long corridor while Julianne held his son snugly to her.

"Please, Lord, please let Nora be all right. Please bring her fever down. Please, Lord," Julianne whispered her prayer under her breath as she closed her eyes and leaned her head back against the chair. "After all he's been through, don't let this be anything too serious. Not now, not one of Luke's children, please. He's already turned his back on You, Lord. Give him reason to trust You again. Let him see Your hand at work in the lives of his kids. And give him peace in this matter—the kind 'that passeth all understanding.'"

Julianne remained in that chair with Todd on her lap until one of her legs began to get a tingling sensation of numbness. Shifting positions didn't ease the problem, so she gathered Todd up in her arms and moved over to a nearby sofa that an elderly couple had just vacated. The cushions were cheap orange vinyl and didn't look very comfortable for sleeping, so Julianne removed her brown sweater vest and placed it on one end of the sofa. Then she laid Todd down with his face resting on the soft material instead of the cold, cracked vinyl. The move didn't disturb the child, and he kept on sleeping there next to Julianne in the busy hospital waiting room.

The coming and going of patients kept Julianne awake during the two hours she spent sitting there, waiting. To keep her mind off worrying, she prayed not only for Nora, but sporadically for other people she saw entering the emergency room in the early hours of the morning. However, the longer she waited, the more concerned she became. How long could it take to diagnose an ear infection and prescribe some antibiotics?

When Luke finally reappeared with a sleeping, peaceful Nora in his arms, Julianne jumped up from her seat to touch Nora's cheek.

"Luke, she feels cooler. Thank God. What did the doctor say?"

"She'll be all right," Luke assured her. "He checked her over thoroughly and decided it's an ear infection. The medicine has already brought her temperature down some. Are you and Todd okay?"

"Yes, we're fine. He's been asleep the whole time. What took you so long?"

Luke shook his head in frustration before placing a kiss against Nora's temple. "We kept getting interrupted by emergencies. They are understaffed tonight. Too many patients, not enough doctors. And she was so good, Julianne. I just held her quietly, and we waited until the doctor could get back to us. She didn't cry or fuss at all."

Julianne raised a hand to her breast and let out a slow sigh of relief. "Thank God everything turned out all right. So, she can go home with us? Now?"

"Yes. I'm supposed to bring her back if she doesn't improve tomorrow, but she seems better already," Luke remarked. "Why don't you stay here with the kids while I bring the truck around to pick you up?"

Julianne nodded. "Sure, I'll wait right here for you."

Within minutes, Luke's truck pulled up by the exit doors and he came in to help carry the children. He took Nora from Julianne's arms, freeing her to gather up Todd from his makeshift bed on the emergency room couch. They headed for the vehicle where they tucked the sleeping children safely in their seats.

"What a night...or morning...or whatever this has been," Luke commented. He guided the truck from the parking area out onto the road. "A cup of coffee sounds good. Let's go through that drive-through." He guided the truck up to place an order. "Coffee for you?"

"How about iced tea? I'm really thirsty," she replied.

"Probably from all of that praying," Luke commented with a brief grin. Then he was placing an order and paying for the drinks which prevented Julianne from responding immediately. And she was grateful. Her first reaction to his remark was feeling hurt, as though he were poking fun at something she regarded as serious, sacred even. But, at the same time, she doubted that he meant it in that way. The Luke she'd come to know didn't seem like the kind of man who would take something like prayer lightly—whether he personally placed much faith in it or not.

Luke pulled the truck into a parking spot on the restaurant lot and turned in his seat to check on the children. They were still sleeping peacefully, so he returned his attention to the cup of coffee in his hand, removing the lid. Steam rose into the warm night air.

"I really appreciate your prayers, Julianne. They were exactly what Nora needed tonight...and something I couldn't give her."

The sudden sense of relief swept over her. She'd been right. He wouldn't make fun of something she held dear. "But, Luke, you could pray for her, too, if you wanted to. There's nothing stopping you... except maybe you, yourself. If you'd just give it a try..."

He raised his gaze to meet Julianne's wide-eyed plea. "I can't. Not now." Then one corner of his mouth turned up into a sad smile. "I'd place more confidence in your prayers than in mine anyday. Yours are a safer bet."

It was the tenderness in his expression that caught her attention. Julianne had expected defensiveness, maybe bitterness, not this wistful sadness she found in his gaze. For a few seconds, Julianne couldn't think of an appropriate response. In fact, her mind went completely blank except for the realization of how very much she liked this gentle, contemplative man sitting next to her.

Then Luke's quiet laugh drew her attention to the curve of his mouth. "You probably haven't heard the words *prayer* and *safe bet* used together in a sentence recently.''

''Not a likely combination.'' She agreed as they shared a smile. ''I guess I never know what to expect from you, Luke O'Hara.''

But what Julianne didn't know was that Luke knew increasingly less about what to expect of himself these days, especially when it came to his newly developing feelings for the young teacher seated next to him on the front seat of his pickup. She was too young, too religious, too optimistic for him and, yet, he'd needed her calm presence tonight almost as much as his little girl had. ''Julianne, I was upset, worried—downright scared for Nora when we arrived at that hospital tonight.'' He paused. ''You know how sick she was, how high her fever was. But then, standing back in the examining room with the doctor, a sense of calm came over me, a kind of peace like I've not known in a while.'' He looked into Julianne's eyes for a long moment. ''Did you pray for that, too?''

She nodded her head.

''I thought so.'' Luke smiled a little. ''Thank you.''

''You're welcome,'' she said when she could find her voice again. ''Praying for you like that, it seemed to be the best way I could help you.''

''You help me in more ways than you know, Julianne. More ways than you know.'' Luke forced himself to look away from her out into the well-lit parking lot. ''We'd better get the kids home. It's been a long night, and it will be time for their Saturday morning cartoons before long."

Julianne raised her cup to her mouth and took her first sip of iced tea. "You're going to be tired tomorrow if you don't get some sleep."

"And so will you." Luke started the truck and eased the vehicle out of the lot and back onto the main road leading home.

"But I'm going home to an empty apartment in which I can sleep as long as I want. You, however, will be contending with one sick child who needs your attention and one healthy child who will be well-rested and ready to play." She took another drink. "Think you can handle it?"

"I don't have much choice, so I guess I can."

"You weren't planning to work today?"

"Only if you call building a new swing set working."

"You bought one. That's great!" Julianne said. "It's exactly what they need for the backyard, Luke, but I just didn't say anything about it."

"Next time you think something like that, say it," Luke responded. "I might not always figure these things out all by myself, you know."

Julianne glanced back at the kids. "You're doing fine with them, Luke. Honestly. You don't need my advice."

"I'm not that good at this single parent life-style, Julianne. I appreciate any and all advice along the way, but go easy on the criticism. I don't always handle that so well. Just ask Maggie."

Julianne turned slightly in her seat to study his

profile through the darkness. "Maggie has nothing but good things to say about you. You know that, don't you?"

"Maggie is a devoted sister. She practically moved in with us after Kimberly died. I don't know what I would have done without her."

Julianne swallowed. Was he ready to talk about Kimberly now? And was she ready to listen? "I'm glad Maggie was there for you," she said quietly. "It must have been a horrible experience."

Luke was silent for a moment, and she wondered if she'd overstepped her boundaries. He was becoming a good friend; she didn't want to injure that part of their relationship.

"*Unimaginable*, might be an appropriate word," Luke finally responded. "Kind of like a nightmare you just can't wake up from."

There was a long silence between them, during which Julianne reached back to feel Nora's forehead. "She's cooler," she commented and Luke made a quiet response that he was glad before slipping back into the silence that had slowly engulfed them. And it was a silence Julianne let stand. Luke was lost in thought, maybe even in old feelings and there was no place for her there. Her place was in the present, helping the twins in whatever way she could. Their father would have to find his own way out of the past.

Tucking the children securely back into their own beds in the wee hours of the morning was a relief. Luke gave them each a light kiss and headed toward his own room for an hour or two of sleep. He had insisted on dropping Julianne at her apartment and waiting until she was safely inside rather than let her drive her own car home from his house at such an unreasonable hour. She could pick it up later in the day, after the sun came up, he'd explained. And wouldn't she enjoy seeing him try to put that new swing set together that afternoon? It might be interesting, he hinted, especially considering he'd never tackled that particular challenge before. So Julianne agreed.

Luke lay down on his bed, exhausted but relieved. Nora would heal, eventually. Life would get back to normal. Normal? What was normal about a man his age raising two preschoolers by himself? But he was too tired to wonder about much of anything for very long.

"Daddy! Daddy!" The cry awakened Luke instantly several hours later, and he was up and in the kids' room in moments.

"You okay?" he asked Nora, reaching to pick her up. "Are you feeling better?"

"Yes. I'm hungry, Daddy. Can we have cereal now?"

Luke ran a hand through his disheveled hair. "Yep. You sure can, honey."

"C'mon, Nora," Todd called to his sister after he hopped out of bed and ran toward the hallway. "It's Saturday! Cartooons!" And he was down the stairs and in front of the television before Luke could greet him with a "good morning." Nora squirmed out of her father's arms and followed quickly in her brother's footsteps.

"She's feeling better," Luke said to himself as she disappeared from his view. He knew he had medicine to give her and breakfast to fix, but first he headed toward the bathroom to shave. Luke had no more than washed his face and squirted shaving cream into the palm of his hand when Nora reappeared upstairs, sticking her head into the bathroom.

"Daddy? Could Julianne be our new mommy?"

Luke, stunned by her request, set the can of shaving cream on the sink and looked down at his little girl. "No, honey. Julianne is your teacher."

"She's your friend."

That was hard to argue with. "Yes, she's a friend to all of us, but—"

"Then why can't she be with us? Like she was last night? At the hospital? All the time?"

"She just can't," Luke responded. He knelt to look into Nora's inquisitive eyes and searched for the correct words. "For Julianne to live here, to be your new mother, she'd have to become my wife."

"So?" Nora placed her hands on her hips as she must have seen her aunt Maggie do dozens of times.

Luke gave a quiet laugh of surprise, mostly. "So I'd need to marry her, Nora. And I'm not planning to marry anyone again. Ever," he added. Shocked at the gravity of his words, he had to stop and think. At thirty-five, he was certainly sentencing himself to a lonely life. But after he'd lost Kimberly, that was the decision he had made, for a combination of reasons, the main one involving the raising of his children. He needed to devote his energy to making up to them for what they'd lost. Squeezing time out to develop a romantic relationship certainly didn't fit into the picture of his daily life. He was barely handling the essentials well enough now. Where would be the free evenings to spend with a woman? Then it occurred to him he was no longer thinking in terms of never finding such a woman. He was now merely lamenting the lack of time to pursue a future with one. And which one wasn't too hard to figure out. This definitely was not the direction he wanted to go.

"Why don't you go downstairs with Todd and watch cartoons?" Wasn't that what kids were supposed to do on Saturday mornings? Luke stood up and, picking up a razor, attempted to continue his morning routine. "We'll talk about this later, Nora."

"With Julianne?"

"No, not with Julianne. Now, scoot. Go see what your brother is watching."

Nora's persistence subsided, and she went to join Todd in the living room. Using the television for a baby-sitter wasn't a good idea, Luke knew too well; but he wanted to get his daughter off the subject of a new mother. That seemed the easiest way to do it. He turned on the water to rinse his razor. It would have broken Kimberly's heart to think of her little girl picking out her replacement. It would break any mother's heart. Wouldn't it?

"No." He could almost hear Maggie say it. Kimberly would want what was best for the children. Those were her exact words regarding Luke and the twins leaving their home in Chicago for the quiet community of Fairweather to be closer to Maggie and Frank. That's what she would say about a new woman in their lives. And Julianne would be the female Maggie had in mind.

Marriage? Now? Luke thought he must be too tired to think clearly. After all, the experience at the emergency room and such a small amount of sleep could have a way of doing that to a person. How could he get married again? He wasn't in love with Julianne, and she certainly wasn't in love with him. They barely knew each other.

Luke finished getting ready for the day and descended the stairs, heading for the kitchen. He reached for bowls and the kids' favorite cereal, which Julianne had brought for them one day when she was there. She was great with the children, Luke had to admit, and they were crazy about her. No, it was more than that. It was something real, and it had started that first day in her classroom. He'd known it almost from the beginning. His kids had gone to her too easily when they first met her. That morning, he'd just been relieved he could leave them somewhere and go to work without being made to feel guilty about all of their crying and pleading. But something practically miraculous had taken place that day, if only he'd acknowledge it.

"Daddy? Can we have cereal?"

"Coming up," he answered. Within moments, he had taken breakfast in to the twins so they could eat at the coffee table like they did most Saturday mornings.

"Is Julianne coming today?" Todd asked.

Luke glanced out the front window toward Julianne's vehicle which remained parked in front of his house. "She'll come to pick up her car. Maybe she can stay and help us build the swing set." Having Julianne around lately had been wonderful for the kids. Not that he hadn't enjoyed her company, too. Very much.

"Can she be our mommy?" Nora raised the question again.

Only this time, Luke was beginning to see a glimmer of possibility. But, still, he couldn't imagine anyone as young and lovely as Julianne being willing to sacrifice her freedom to raise another woman's children. She had her whole life ahead of her, plenty of time to wait for the right guy, to fall in love and have babies of her own when the time came. A marriage to Luke would be one of convenience—his convenience—he knew. What would she have to gain by agreeing to such a union?

"I love her," Todd added without taking his eyes off his favorite superhero who was now flying across the blue sky of the television.

"Me, too," Nora quickly chimed in. "Let's marry her."

Luke returned his attention to the children. They were Kimberly's children, yes. But his, too. And the responsibility of caring for them had fallen on him alone, unless he found someone to share it with. And, at the moment, Julianne Quinn was the only possibility he'd be willing to consider.

"Let's eat breakfast," Luke suggested. "Then we'll go out back and decide where the new swing set should be placed. Maybe Julianne will come over and help.'' But help him...what? Raise his kids? Luke shook his head. He wasn't one for crazy notions like this. Maybe he should have a cup of coffee and get back to reality. A man with his responsibilities, his past, his empty heart wouldn't be much of a match for someone like Julianne Quinn. He was probably foolish to allow the thought to even cross his mind, and he walked from the room without the children even noticing. Reaching for the can of coffee, he measured several tablespoons and dumped it into the coffeemaker. That's when the phone rang.

''Hello,'' he said as he switched on the coffeemaker.

''Hi. How's Nora?''

Luke smiled. The voice was Julianne's he knew, even though it sounded a little strained or scratchy. ''She's fine. No fever this morning.''

''And how are you?'' she asked.

''Tired. You don't sound so good yourself. Are you feeling okay?'' He didn't want her to get sick. What would happen if she did? At the center or at home?

''I'm fine.'' She cleared her throat. ''I haven't talked yet this morning. That's why I sound funny. Hold on a second.''

Luke heard a few noises in the background, but she returned to the phone within moments.

''I had to get my cup out of the microwave. I can barely function without my morning tea, you know.''

''No,'' he replied with a subtle laugh. ''I didn't know that about you, Julianne. The next time I drag you out in the middle of the night to help take care of my kids, I'll make sure you get your morning cup of tea.''

"Thank you, sir," she answered playfully. "It would be much appreciated, I assure you. So, Nora's really, truly okay today?"

"As unbelievable as that sounds after last night, yes, she is. She's eating breakfast right now."

"Did you get the medicine in her yet?"

"No, but I will as soon as I hang up. I didn't forget, I just haven't gotten around to it yet." He'd had too much on his mind—like his family's future. And Julianne's. "Your car is still out here."

"I know. I thought I'd walk over to get it later this morning. Will you be home?"

"We'll most likely be in the backyard working on the swing set. Come back and join us if you have time."

Julianne had time. Too much time to satisfy her. Another Saturday cooped up in her apartment alone definitely was not what she had in mind. "I was thinking of maybe taking the twins off your hands for a couple of hours, so you could get some sleep. If you're interested."

"Let's see how things progress with the construction project first. That could take all day."

"I doubt it."

"I've never put one of these things together before. Trust me, Julianne, it could be a lengthy ordeal. So, I can tell the kids you're coming?"

"Yes," she answered. "I'll be there soon."

Luke informed the children of their plans, which

roused great excitement from them both as they jumped up and down on the couch. It made him wonder briefly if their Saturdays with only Dad were boring in comparison. They certainly came to life when Julianne was involved in anything they did. The attention of their gentle, caring teacher did wonders for them. Maybe, Luke considered, if he could only open his own heart a little…

The cool flicker of apprehension coursed through him. No, he didn't need, didn't want, couldn't afford that kind of vulnerability again. Someday, maybe. Later—when the kids were older. Years from now—maybe—when the pain of loss wasn't still so fresh. Reverend Hunter was doing fine on his own even after all this time, and Maggie had said it'd been three years since he'd lost his fiancée in a car accident. Three years. Luke thought he would need all of that—maybe more—before he could feel again. And, even then, it wouldn't seem right. What was fair about Kimberly being gone and he, himself, going on? Living, loving, enjoying life? What right did he have to know these things without her? The wall of defense against happiness that Luke had erected was doing its job well. But, he wondered for probably the first time, what would life be like for his son and daughter if their father had a cold, empty heart?

A burst of Julianne's undiluted laughter filled the air unexpectedly, and silly giggles from the twins joined in the amusement.

"It can't possibly be right, Luke," Julianne managed to say while trying to suppress another laugh. "Look at all of the leftover pieces." In a pile on the ground were lots of nuts, bolts and screws that Luke had the sinking feeling should have been included in the crooked swing set he'd just completed constructing.

"I see them, Julianne, but they might be extras. Maybe the company packed too much hardware in the box when they shipped it out. I honestly didn't find any place to put them."

"Maybe the fact that you drilled your own holes in the poles..."

"The precut ones didn't line up," Luke reminded her with a grimace. "I didn't have any choice if I wanted to get this swing set together today."

"Maybe we should take it back—" Julianne started to say.

"No! Not our new swing set!" Nora and Todd protested.

"To return it, I'd have to take this thing apart and get it back in that box," Luke remarked. He took a quick survey of the painstaking work that would be involved. "I don't have enough patience for that, Julianne."

"No, probably not. Especially considering it's taken—" she took a slow, dramatic look at her watch "—five hours to get this far with it." Julianne tried to act serious for the moment, but she couldn't keep her mouth from twitching with amusement.

"Lucky for you that you have such a pretty smile," came Luke's offhand remark with a trace of laughter in his voice. "Otherwise, it would be hard to forgive you for being so amused by all of this."

Julianne stood up from where she'd been seated on the back steps and walked over to the metal framework. Placing a hand on one of the poles, she shook it to test its sturdiness. "It seems surprisingly steady, Luke. Really." She glanced in his direction with a teasing slant to her mouth and found him approaching her with a glint of humor in his blue eyes.

When he'd covered the space between them in a few long strides, he reached toward the same pole Julianne held on to. He gripped the space right above her slender fingers, his warm, strong hand touching hers although he hadn't really meant to do that. Julianne didn't move as Luke tried to shake the pole loose, too, without success.

"I guess it's steadier than it looks," he stated. But all humor faded from his expression when he looked into Julianne's delicate face only to find her eyes brimming with unexpected emotion. Practically of its own volition, Luke's hand slid down to cover hers on the metal pole. Julianne was close enough to slip his arms around. To embrace. Fully. Easily. And the smell of her light perfume clouded his thinking. He'd kissed her before. He knew how it could be. The warm memory he'd tried to block out, burned brightly in its return. Luke raised a hand to touch the silky hair that hung freely around Julianne's face, and he heard the lovely sound of her breath catching in her throat. And all logic was lost. Luke cupped the back of her head with one hand, drawing her to him as they leaned together.

"Daddy, Daddy. You're in the way! We want to swing," Nora said, rushing toward her father, bumping into him and unintentionally ending the tender moment just as it was unfolding. Both startled adults glanced down at the giggling little girl.

Julianne raised her hand to her mouth and laughed lightly, nervously at the abrupt interruption as Luke released her. He'd gone from leaning toward her for a kiss they both needed to being unexpectedly grabbed around the legs by his daughter. He exhaled a quiet sigh before turning his attention to his kids. He picked up Nora with maybe just a hint of relief. She'd saved him from a long bout of guilt. For that, he should be grateful. But, on the other hand, he could handle a little guilt for the right reasons. Luke glanced over at Julianne who was walking with Todd, hand in hand toward the back door, heading into the house for some unspecified reason. He wished she'd look back. He wished he could know her thoughts about the kiss they'd shared, and the ones they hadn't.

"Daddy, can I swing? Please?"

"Let me work on straightening this thing up first, honey. Then you may." Luke spent the next several minutes tightening bolts, readjusting some alignments and getting the swing set into usable condition for the twins. Still, after all of his improvements, he wasn't totally satisfied.

By then, Julianne and Todd had returned from the kitchen with glasses of lemonade and a plate of fresh fruit. Nora was the first one to bite into a section of an orange, and as the juice ran down the girl's chin,

Julianne doubted the wisdom of bringing such a messy snack out for them. She probably should have gone for the peanut butter cookies instead. Then Luke's words cut through her thoughts.

"I don't know, Julianne. I'm still not sure about the safety of this swing set," Luke commented. He took the glass of lemonade she offered, but noticed she avoided meeting his gaze. Instead, she concentrated on Todd's peeling of half a banana. But Luke continued, "Maybe I'll ask Warren Sinclair to take a look at it one evening this week. He can build just about anything. He should know whether or not this will stand the test of time and use by four-year-olds."

Julianne looked up at the mention of the name. "That's an excellent idea, Luke. We'd both feel better if he checked it out before the kids use it much. But I didn't realize you knew Warren."

"Maggie introduced us over at the day care one afternoon. He was there to take Betty Anderson out to dinner, and she was running late. So Warren and I started talking about some of the boats he'd built." Luke began gathering his tools and cleaning up the mess generated by their afternoon project. "Well, I've had much better Saturdays than this one," he commented.

"I haven't," Julianne remarked with quiet sincerity.

Her response immediately captured Luke's attention, and his gaze returned to Julianne and lingered there as she and the children finished eating apple slices and grapes. Luke's Saturdays would immediately be much improved, if she'd agree to share them with him. All of them. Then he looked away. How could he be thinking such a thing? A young, beautiful woman sat on the back steps to his house at this moment, enjoying his children, true, but what would make him think she might want to do this permanently? Day in and day out, with no promise of love from him? Luke wasn't sure he'd ever have that to offer again to any woman. Loyalty, yes; commitment, definitely. But love? Real love? Somehow, he didn't feel entitled to that anymore.

"Luke?" Julianne spoke his name gently. She'd finally gathered enough boldness to look directly at him, risking his recognition of the play of emotion he would likely see in her eyes. Immediately, she noticed the deepening lines of concentration along his brow and his melancholy frown. "Are you okay?" she asked softly.

He gave her a distracted nod and went back to picking up the items in the yard. The large sections of cardboard box, he slid into the garage for temporary storage rather than have a gust of wind send them sailing down the street. Dropping his wrenches and screwdriver back into his toolbox, he stood in the silence of the garage momentarily. It was cool and quiet, and he felt very alone. Not that it was a new feeling for him. It followed him around like a shadow, from dawn until dusk and beyond. Except, sometimes, like today, when Julianne was with them. He could almost feel that he belonged with someone again. "No," he corrected his thinking aloud to himself in the solitude of the building, "not just someone. With her."

Chapter Six

"I'm going to ask Julianne to marry me," Luke stated quietly, then looked in Maggie's direction for a reaction. "What do you think my chances are?"

"For a yes?" Maggie asked with a sly smile. "Pretty good, I'd say. But aren't you rushing things a bit? You've known each other such a short while."

"I realize it's not perfect timing," Luke remarked with a sigh. "And she's so young and spirited, and she has such confidence about life. Maybe I'd be taking too much away from her by marrying her."

"That would be something only Julianne could answer. When are you planning to propose to her? And how?"

Now, it was Luke's turn to smile. "How? Getting kind of nosy, aren't you, little sister?"

But Maggie was deadly serious. "Julianne had her heart broken not long ago by her college boyfriend. I think she deserves a better go at it this time. She's a Christian, Luke, and regardless of your personal beliefs or disbeliefs, she wants to remain one. Marriage for her may mean something entirely different from what it means for you right now." Maggie was silent for a moment before adding. "Don't start something you can't finish."

"Meaning what?" Luke asked, honestly mystified by his sister's remark. "That I might ask her and then not go through with it?"

"That you might marry her for convenience now, then find someone else you want later. Julianne would be crushed by a divorce, Luke. If that in any way could be a possibility—"

"It's not, Maggie. I wouldn't do that to Julianne." He was silent for a moment. He'd never hurt her that way. "Marriage is forever."

"Marriage is until 'death do us part,'" Maggie corrected.

A shadow of certainty crossed Luke's face, and he turned to look out into the starry summer sky. "No, in some ways, it's forever." His mind went back to Kimberly and their beginning. Neither had been Christians when they'd met, and they'd lived together for nearly a year before deciding to make it legal. They'd given their lives to Christ during a huge crusade that had come through the Chicago area several years before the twins were born. That's when their lives had changed. Their plans, their goals, their futures. Until Kimberly became ill.

"You could live another fifty years," Maggie reminded her brother. "Kimberly wouldn't want you to go through life alone. It's okay to let yourself have feelings for Julianne.''

"I like Julianne. Very much. But feelings aren't what this marriage is about. The twins need a mother, and Julianne would be a wonderful one. She loves them already. I can see it in her eyes—the way they light up when she's with them." Luke studied Maggie's definite frown. "It will be a marriage of convenience, sis. It's too soon for it to be more—for either of us.''

"But, Luke, have you ever held her hand, kissed her...anything?" Maggie asked in exasperation. "A little romance would be good for both of you. Julianne is a lovely young woman.''

"I'm very aware of that." Too aware sometimes, he thought. "And, yes, we've kissed.''

"And?''

"And, I felt like I was cheating on my wife. Is that what you want to hear, Maggie?" Luke retorted and stood up from the step where he'd been seated. He raked a hand through his dark hair. "I care very much for Julianne. If she agrees to marry me, I think our relationship can grow into something more than an arrangement to provide for my children, eventually. But it's too soon for that now. For both of us. She's very young, and she barely knows me.''

Maggie stood up, leaving the porch swing to sway back and forth without her as she walked over to where Luke stood and slipped her arm through his. "I love you, and I love Julianne. I think you'd be a perfect match, Luke, in every regard. If you'd open your eyes to it, you'd see that this relationship could be a healing for all four of you. Accept it, embrace it and be grateful.''

''I am,'' Luke said quietly, raising his eyes toward the heaven he used to pray to. ''I am, Maggie. In my own way.''

She nodded. Then with a smile and a squeeze of her brother's arm, she motioned toward her front door. ''And I'm a tired, old pregnant woman who has to get some sleep or I won't be fit for anything tomorrow.'' Maggie patted her tummy affectionately.

Luke nodded and walked to the front door with his sister. ''Let me see what Uncle Frank has the kids doing in here.''

''Oh, I know,'' Maggie said quickly. ''He has a stack of new children's books that came in this week for the Book-Stop. He was going to read some of them to the twins to see which ones they liked best. He's hoping to sell some to Betty Anderson for our use at the center.''

''So, Nora and Todd are his guinea pigs for this test,'' Luke remarked just as his children came running from the downstairs family room.

''Daddy! Daddy! Uncle Frank has these great books. You've gotta see them,'' Nora was saying as she ran into her father's arms. Todd was not far behind his sister.

''Let's take a quick look, then we need to get going. It's past your bedtime already.''

So Luke saw the books about Thanksgiving, Christmas and snowy days before they headed home for the night. Walking home would have been pleasant, but as he pulled the truck into their driveway, he was glad he'd driven. It was easier for the kids. Parking up close to the garage, he carried a sleepy Nora while Todd walked along beside him chattering about the games he'd played at the center that day. The kids seemed happy there, in Julianne's group. Having her with them, living with them, as a part of their family, could only raise the quality of their lives. Nora and Todd needed her.

Luke adjusted the air conditioner in the kids' room and placed their stuffed animals next to them in their beds. Nora reached for her bunny and held it tightly, but Todd was snoring by then and the little basset hound would have to be satisfied sleeping beside his master tonight, rather than in his grip.

Luke smiled at his children. They really did look like angels when they slept. But they wouldn't look quite so heavenly eight hours from now, and Luke was tired so he turned to head for his own room. He paused for a moment to look out a window into the darkness. The kids needed Julianne, but so did Luke, he knew. There was a gentleness about her that could take the edge off the coldness he too often felt. Maggie was right; he should be grateful for her presence in their lives, and he was. He just wasn't ready to tell God about it. Yet.

"Julianne..." Luke began, then stopped. He moistened his dry lips and looked down at the floor, trying to remember the words he'd rehearsed. He'd tried to recall how he'd proposed to Kimberly when it occurred to him, he hadn't actually asked her to marry him. They'd simply come to that decision during a discussion and agreed to marry. It had been simple, practical. A little like this time, maybe? He looked back into Julianne's wide brown eyes as she patiently waited for him to continue. No, this was nothing like that. Julianne was younger, hopeful, more optimistic. This was never going to work. She'd want something romantic and promising. She'd want loving and caring and tenderness she wouldn't find in him because it wasn't there anymore. This was a mistake. "Let's go get something to eat. Frank has the kids—"

"But, Luke," she interrupted, "I thought you wanted to talk to me about something. Without the kids, I mean."

He was in too deep to get out now. Maggie may have even told Julianne what he had in mind, so he may as well proceed. He would let her say no, and get it over with. "Julianne, I know we haven't known each other very long...but, I feel comfortable with you. I like you. Very much."

Her mouth curved into a small, shy smile. "I like you, too, Luke." Probably a little too much at times, she thought, for no more than she actually knew about him.

"And the kids love you," he added. "And, I know you love them. I can see it in your eyes when you're with them."

"They're easy to love. They're wonderful kids. Honestly. Being with them five days a week is a pleasure."

"How much of that pleasure do you think you can stand?" he asked quietly. Now, there was a statement he hadn't planned to use. He watched Julianne's eyes blink in bewilderment.

"What do you mean? I love Nora and Todd. I could be with them every day."

"Would you? Be with them every day?"

She shrugged. "I'd love to, but I'm not sure I understand what you're getting at. Do you need a weekend baby-sitter?"

Luke took a deep breath, then exhaled. Here goes, he thought. "I need a wife, Julianne, and my children need a mother." He studied the flash of amazement that lit her eyes. She obviously hadn't seen this coming; Maggie must not have mentioned it to her. "Would you consider...Julianne...will you marry me?"

"Marry?" Julianne sat down on the sofa. "We haven't known each other very long."

"I realize that," Luke acknowledged before he sank down beside her on the sofa in his living room. "I'm not asking for more than...a marriage of convenience for now, Julianne. Nora and Todd adore you, and everything, all of our lives would be so much better if you'd become a part of it. I know, I realize that you're very young and that you deserve better than this."

"Luke, I'd never think such a thing. You're a wonderful man. I care very much for you. And I love the kids." She did care for him far more than she'd ever shown. But marriage? "I'd have to think about this. Pray about it. This is a huge decision, Luke." Julianne stood up and moved away from him. Walking toward the front window, she rubbed her hands against her arms to dispel a sudden chill.

"It is a huge decision. I know. And you can take all the time you need to think it over. But you will think about it?" he asked with his hopefulness evident in those blue eyes that Julianne was coming dangerously close to loving. She only wished Luke could feel the same about her.

"Yes, of course, I'll think about it." And, little else, she knew as she turned the thought over in her mind. Marriage to Luke. Two children to love. Kids who would be hers to raise. This could be the answer to her prayers. She longed to be a mother; maybe the Lord was opening this door, opening Luke's heart up to her. It was possible, wasn't it? If she could be patient, Luke could learn to love her in time.

He got up from the sofa and went to Julianne's side. His hand squeezed her shoulder in a tender touch. "Take your time. Talk to Maggie about this if it would be helpful. I won't say anything to the children. Not until you've made a decision."

She turned to look into his face. Falling in love with Luke O'Hara could be so easy if only she'd let herself. But she wanted some sign from him, something to encourage her, something worth waiting for. "Luke, I don't know what to say."

"Don't say anything now. Just think it over and let me know your decision once it's made," Luke said. "And I hope it's yes." He couldn't help but want this woman in his life. Her companionship, her affection, her warmth. Her presence was what he needed to make him whole again; Julianne could offer him that. If he couldn't find contentment with her, then it probably wasn't to be found anywhere in this lifetime. But that was too much to tell her now. Or was it? "Julianne, if you'll marry me, if you give us time, we could make a good life together. This can be more than an arrangement, someday, if you want it to be...when we're both ready."

She nodded, sinking her teeth into the fleshy inside of her cheek as she listened to him talk. He cared for her; she could feel it in even his casual touch. Maybe time was all they needed. That and God's help. "I'll give you an answer, Luke. Soon. I promise."

He nodded again and extended a hand to Julianne. She smiled and slipped her slender hand into his, allowing their fingers to link together in mutual warmth. The hopeful, faintly eager look in Luke's eyes left a lingering ache in Julianne's heart, and, in that moment, she couldn't imagine her life without this man. Or his children. How could she tell him no? But was she ready to say yes?

Luke's voice brought her back to reality. "Frank won't be able to handle the kids alone for very long, and Maggie wasn't home when I left them. She'd gone shopping for baby clothes. Let's get a quick sandwich on the way over there," he suggested.

So, talk of a marriage was concluded for the moment while they enjoyed roast beef sandwiches and homemade vegetable soup at the deli on the village green. They talked about the children, then Luke's business, Julianne's work at the day care and Maggie's fragile health.

"I keep praying everything will work out for her,

Luke," Julianne stated, then wiped her mouth lightly with a paper napkin. "It just has to this time. Maggie's waited so long for this baby."

"You have far too much faith for your own good," Luke remarked quietly before taking a sip of his coffee.

"But without faith, what do we hold on to? What do we have?" she asked.

"Reality," he answered. "That's the best thing to hold on to because it's what you face in the end."

The sadness was back in Luke's expression, not that it surprised Julianne much. This talk would raise thoughts of his past, and it was those thoughts that threatened the future they might have together. Her eyes misted with tears. She didn't relish the idea of facing that struggle for the rest of her life. Past versus present; trust versus doubt. Careful thinking about this marriage was what she needed, rather than acting on her feelings. She needed to talk to someone. Reverend Ben, maybe?

Then Luke noticed the anxious look on her face as she sat across the table from him and realized instantly that he'd caused it. "I'm sorry, Julianne. I shouldn't have said that. Maggie is your best friend. You have every reason to want the best for her."

"Let's go get the children," she said suddenly. "It's getting late."

Luke stood up and reached for his wallet. He'd said the wrong thing, he knew. But he meant what he'd said, even if the timing wasn't the best. He paid for their food and turned to open the door for her, but Julianne pulled the heavy door open by herself and stepped out into the warmth of the summer evening. Soon Luke joined her on the sidewalk.

"Julianne, I didn't mean to upset you. I just meant—" He stopped. What did he mean? That he didn't believe in God or prayer or help from above? No, that wasn't it. Not exactly.

"You meant that you don't trust the Lord. I thought you'd think differently now, after Nora being so sick the other night. God helped her—through us, Luke. He helped us get her to the hospital, He helped the doctor know what to do, He helped the medicine bring her fever down."

"You're more idealistic than I am, Julianne. More trusting, more optimistic. You believe in God in a way I learned not to do."

Julianne was walking away from him, quickly, and it took several long strides for Luke to catch up to her. He reached for her arm, grabbing it and stopping her in her tracks. She pivoted to look him squarely in the face. "If you want your children raised to love God, then you'd better stop being so openly critical of Him. You could destroy their beliefs the same as you've destroyed your own."

"Me? I didn't do anything except ask for something."

"And God said no." Julianne pulled her arm away and sank her hands into the pockets of her long skirt. "Sometimes He does, Luke. I'm very sorry that you lost your wife, and I don't know why it happened. But it did. Every answer from God isn't yes. The Lord isn't a great big Santa Claus in the sky that gives us everything we want. We don't always know what's best for us.''

"And He does?'' Luke countered quietly, angrily. "That's what we're supposed to accept, isn't it?''

"That's what the Bible teaches, and I believe what the Bible teaches. I want Nora and Todd to believe it, too. I can help them grow up that way. Isn't that what you want from me? To raise your children, Kimberly's children as Christians?'' She watched the color drain from Luke's face as he stared at her, complete surprise on his face.

"Yes...no...'' he stammered, then raised a hand to his forehead as his mind raced. He wanted so much more from her than that. "I want my children to be your children, Julianne. They need you, they love you.''

She blinked back angry tears and looked across the village green toward some children playing soccer. "I love Nora and Todd,'' she quietly admitted. "Very much. Too much.'' Pulling a hand from her pocket, she wiped at a trickle of tears with the back of her hand.

"No,'' Luke stated and reached toward her again, touching her arm much more gently this time. "Don't ever think it's too much. They need all the love you can give, Julianne.'' *So do I.* The words flashed through his mind from somewhere deep inside, but he wouldn't let them out. He couldn't ask her for something he, himself, wasn't willing to give. "I'll—I'll try to be more respectful of your beliefs. I want the kids to go to church, to trust God the way I used to. I won't do anything to hurt that.''

Julianne looked down at the strong hand that held her arm, and Luke released her. But she didn't turn away from him as he half expected her to do. She simply saw an opportunity to ask something of him and took it. "Would you attend church with us, occasionally? For the children's sake?" she asked.

Luke's bleak, tight-lipped expression didn't change as he nodded his head. "Occasionally," he agreed. He'd do whatever it would take to have her in their lives. He had to, because at this point, he couldn't imagine going on without her. "Just don't expect an immediate, miraculous transformation in me."

Julianne's mouth curved into a spontaneous smile. "I didn't ask for a miracle. I just want to be able to sit in church with you and the kids as a family, if we decide to become a family, I mean."

Luke's strained expression relaxed into a smile. "That decision is already made as far as I'm concerned. The rest is up to you." He wanted an answer from her—now—but the uncertainty in her dark eyes warned him not to expect one yet. There was much about him she didn't know, and she obviously hadn't been happy with what had transpired here tonight. Although, the outcome seemed to have satisfied her, Luke reminded himself. And, somehow, he'd managed to commit himself to attending church again, at least once in a while. He hadn't planned on that figuring into their arrangement.

"Luke, I didn't mean to get so upset with you." Julianne's quiet voice sounded very apologetic.

"No," he objected. "I deserved it. Let's go get

the kids. They'll be happy to see you again.'' He extended his hand in a peace offering, and watched her hesitantly slide her hand inside his to receive a reassuring squeeze. ''I think Nora and Todd get jealous of me when I have you all to myself for very long. They seem to think you belong to them.''

Julianne swallowed back the words she longed to say. She wanted to belong to them—and to Luke. But she needed him to want that, too. And, tonight, she was beginning to believe maybe he really did.

''C'mon,'' Luke said with an easy pull of her hand. ''We've left poor Frank alone long enough. He's not used to being with them without Maggie's help. He could be tied up and stuffed in a closet by now.''

Julianne laughed quietly as she walked close beside Luke on their way toward the Wren's house which was not far from the village green. ''I don't think the twins are quite capable of overpowering Uncle Frank yet.''

''Probably not, but I wouldn't put anything past Nora. She's going to be a woman of action, or haven't you noticed her take-charge attitude?''

''I've noticed,'' Julianne agreed. ''And Todd's a sweetheart. He just goes along with whatever she says.''

''He may as well get used to it,'' Luke remarked with another squeeze to her hand. ''It's pretty much the way of the world.''

''That's not true,'' she protested, ''although the world might be in much better shape if women did make the decisions.''

"Is this a warning as to what kind of a partnership you would expect our marriage to be?" Luke asked curiously. *Our marriage.* The words sounded good to him. He wondered if she noticed.

She smiled. "I don't know yet. I guess a fifty-fifty partnership is what comes to mind, but I've heard Reverend Ben say that in reality, each partner has to give one hundred percent all the time to make it work."

"Reverend Ben is a smart man," Luke replied. Although, as they continued their walk toward Frank and Maggie's house in the early evening hours, Luke couldn't help but question the pastor's wisdom in letting Julianne Quinn get away. He knew he certainly wouldn't, if the choice was his to make.

Chapter Seven

"Reverend Ben isn't in?" Julianne asked the next morning as she walked into the office shared between the day-care center and The Old First Church.

"Not yet, but soon," Emma Fulton answered. She smiled at Julianne. "Coffee?"

"No, thanks. How are you this morning, Emma? That sweater you have on is beautiful," Julianne commented while approaching the secretary's desk. "Is it new?"

"Yes, it is," Emma replied, her face beaming with a wide grin. She ran her hand down one sleeve of the soft ivory garment. "It was a present from my Sam. He knows the air-conditioning in here has been too cold to suit me these past few days, so he bought this new cardigan for me. It was such a lovely surprise."

"It's very pretty," Julianne responded, "and it is freezing in here. I thought Betty said Warren Sinclair was going to take a look at the air-conditioning this week.''

''He'll be here later today. And Reverend Ben will be in any minute. Do you need to see him?''

''Yes, I was wondering if you would check his schedule to see if he'd have a few minutes to talk to me later? Today, preferably? It wouldn't take long. I just need his opinion on something,'' she said and hoped the secretary wouldn't inquire as to what the subject of the discussion would be. With Emma, that was always a possibility.

Emma smiled and reached for the pastor's appointment book. ''Certainly, Julianne. Just a moment.'' Picking up a pencil, she tapped it absentmindedly on the desk. ''How about right when the center closes today? Six sound okay?''

''Well, yes, but I know how Reverend Ben is about wanting you here in the office during his counseling sessions. I don't want you to have to work late.''

''Don't worry,'' Emma assured her with a shake of her head. ''I'm staying tonight, anyway, to finish up the monthly newsletter, so I'll be right here at my desk. Sam is working overtime at the hardware tonight so it will be a good time to take care of this work I'm behind on. Is six all right then?''

Julianne nodded. ''Yes. I'll be here as soon as the last child leaves. Thank you.'' She tucked some stray hair behind her ear and turned to leave the office.

''Julianne...nothing serious, I hope?'' Emma asked, bringing a reluctant smile to Julianne's face. She'd nearly made it out of the office without Emma

Fulton's curiosity making an appearance. Almost, but not quite.

"No, nothing serious," Julianne responded before disappearing through the doorway. Just the possibility of changing my entire life by marrying Luke O'Hara, she considered as she made her way back to her classroom. Wouldn't Emma be amazed to know there was a marriage proposal Julianne was contemplating? In fact, that piece of news would bring such delight to the matchmaking secretary, Julianne felt a little guilty about her pleasure in keeping the secret.

The day passed rather quickly for Miss Quinn and her students, although their afternoon playtime in the activity room was interrupted once again with a loud thunderstorm. Apparently, they had experienced enough bad weather this summer to be getting used to it because none of the four-year-olds overreacted to the noise. Not even Nora and Todd. However, Julianne was grateful she had Fluffy and Dunkum nearby, just in case. Thank the Lord for stuffed animals, she'd thought more than a few times over the years.

The inclement weather meant Luke's landscaping project in Minneapolis was rained out, so Julianne expected him to stop in early. And she was right. Around four o'clock he showed up to pick up the twins. She and all of her students were seated on the floor wearing their old paint shirts and working on a large finger painting when the classroom door opened. Julianne smiled up at Luke as he entered the room. A sense of peace and satisfaction warmed her heart at the sight of him, but it was shortlived due to the doubts lurking within her. This was the man she might marry...might not marry...might marry. She may as well be picking petals from a daisy. Loves me. Loves me not. No, that wouldn't even work for them, she realized. Love was not in the picture. She looked away hastily, hoping the indecision that wearied her wasn't readable in her expression. Offering a weak, "Hi," she reached for a rag to wipe her hands before she looked up again.

"Hello," Luke responded. His shirt and jeans remained damp from being caught out in the rain, but seeing Julianne took his mind off everything for a moment. Everything except how cautious she looked. Uncertain, uneasy—and lovely.

"You could have gone home and changed clothes before you picked up the kids, you know," Julianne remarked with a gentle shake of her head. "There's no rule that says you have to get them the moment you're finished working."

"I know," he agreed, "but I'm in kind of a hurry. I want to stop in and see how Maggie's doing. I can change later. I'm nearly dry now, anyway."

Julianne stood up and reached for Nora. "C'mon, Nora, let's wash your hands, so you can go with Daddy. Todd, you, too, sweetie. Come on."

Watching Julianne usher the children to the sink in the corner of the room, Luke wondered how she found the patience to do this kind of work. Being with children, encouraging them, teaching them, helping them...all day long, day after day. He'd prefer his own past seven hours of loading and unloading sod over Julianne's workday. It seemed easier.

"Could Julianne come over tonight?" Todd asked while his teacher rubbed his hands together under a stream of warm water. "Please, Daddy?"

"Sure, son," Luke responded. He reached for the kids' backpack hanging on a hook by the door. "Maybe Julianne would like to have tomato soup and grilled cheese sandwiches with us."

"Yes!" Nora exclaimed.

"I'm sorry, but I can't," Julianne explained while helping Nora rinse red paint from her hands. "I have an appointment tonight."

"'Pointment? What's that?" the little girl asked.

"Appointment. It's a meeting," Julianne replied. "I'm supposed to meet with Reverend Ben at six o'clock." She raised her gaze to meet Luke's inquisitive eyes. "I'm sorry. Maybe I could have soup and sandwiches with you another night? Tomorrow, perhaps?"

Luke's smile came easily. "Tomorrow would be good," he responded.

"Are you eating dinner at your 'pointment?" Todd asked. Luke was pleased with his son's question. It came close to the one he wanted to ask.

"No." Julianne pulled a hand towel from the metal bar on the side of the sink. "I'm just going to talk with the pastor for a while. There's no food involved," she added with a grin while drying off the children's clean hands. "There you go. Paint-free and ready to leave with Dad." She felt the weight of Luke's gaze on her and looked in his direction.

He seemed suddenly serious, thoughtful, maybe even worried. She couldn't be sure.

Luke looked away. "C'mon, kids. We've gotta go see Maggie. She wasn't feeling well this morning when I spoke with her."

"Tell her we miss her at the center," Julianne said. "I'll call her tonight." Julianne glanced toward the remaining members of her class and found them happily continuing with their messy artwork with Lisa, her part-time assistant, overseeing the project. Then she watched Nora and Todd run to their father, each child grabbing one of Luke's hands.

"Let's go see Aunt Maggie, Daddy." Then Nora called out to her teacher. "Have fun with your 'pointment."

Julianne smiled and waved goodbye to Luke and the twins as they disappeared through the door. A wave of emptiness washed over her as she watched them go. How easily she could have gone with them.

"Have fun with your 'pointment." Luke considered his daughter's words while he helped the children into the back of the truck. He fastened their seat belts securely, listening to their excited chatter of all they'd done with Julianne that day. The kids loved her. They needed her.

Luke's hope was that Julianne wouldn't have too much fun in her meeting with the young pastor. She was probably planning to discuss Luke's offer of marriage with Reverend Ben, probably wanting to know his opinion, his thoughts on the matter. And Reverend Ben might not be anxious to see her commit her life to someone else. After all, Julianne and

Ben had dated briefly and discovered themselves to be friends. That was all, or so she had said. But if there had been any hint of something beyond friendship, this would be the moment for Ben to speak or "forever hold his peace."

And, as much as Luke hated to admit it, Reverend Ben would be a better match for Julianne than Luke could ever be. Ben wouldn't burden Julianne with his past. Ben had a clean slate. No first wife's shadow to live in, no other woman's children to raise and care for. Luke climbed into the vehicle and started the motor. He could lose Julianne tonight. Without even being near her. Without ever really having her. It didn't seem fair, he thought as he swallowed hard at the lump in his throat. But he wouldn't try to convince her otherwise if she chose Ben over him. He cared too much for her to do that.

Six o'clock finally came around that afternoon. Julianne had hoped to finish up by five-thirty and have time to go over her plans for tomorrow before she went to see Reverend Ben, but she didn't get that chance. One of the parents didn't come to pick up the last remaining four-year-old until six exactly, so Julianne locked up her room and hurried over to the office to meet with the pastor. Emma Fulton was seated at her desk, working her way through the monthly newsletter and a tuna salad sandwich. She looked up when Julianne entered the room.

"Hi, dear. Have a seat. Reverend Ben will be with you in a moment. Wasn't that thunderstorm awful this afternoon?"

"Yes," Julianne agreed before relaxing into the large overstuffed chair in the corner of the office. "But it didn't upset the children much." She thought of Nora and Todd. She'd been very worried about their reaction to the severe weather, but they'd handled it well.

"Even the O'Hara twins?" Emma asked, looking up from her computer with a curious glance. "I remember the last time there was a tornado warning and they cried and cried—"

"Julianne?" Reverend Ben unknowingly interrupted the conversation by bursting in through the side door with a gust of wind. The papers stacked on Emma's desk blew everywhere. "Sorry, Emma," he quickly apologized as he, Emma and Julianne rushed to collect the pages. "I shouldn't have come in that door. I forgot that you'd still be using the computer this late in the afternoon."

"That's all right," Emma assured the pastor as they put the pieces of the monthly newsletter back in a haphazard pile on her desk. "Julianne has been waiting to speak with you. Why don't you go on into your office? I'll finish cleaning up this mess."

"Wow, what a day," Ben remarked while opening the door to his office and ushering Julianne into the room. He switched on the overhead lights. "A tornado touched down over by Baylor's Landing."

"Oh, no!" Julianne exclaimed, raising her hand to her mouth. "Was anyone hurt? Is Betty's home all right? She didn't say anything about it."

Just then the phone buzzed. "Excuse me a minute," Reverend Ben said. "Emma, hold my calls, please."

"But it's that runaway boy, Jason, on the line. Don't you want to take that call?"

"Yes, yes, I do. I'll just be a minute, Julianne." Reverend Ben punched the button for the first line. "Jason? It's good to hear from you. How are you doing?"

Julianne felt as though she were intruding on the conversation, but Ben didn't seem to mind her presence. She walked around his office looking at the various photographs of The Old First Church taken over the years that were displayed on the paneled walls.

"No, I haven't spoken to your parents," Reverend Ben continued. "Not yet. But I'll be glad to do that, if you want me to. Tell me where you're staying. I'll pick you up, we could get a steak somewhere. Maybe talk for a while. No, Jason. You know I can't do that."

There was a long pause while Reverend Ben was apparently listening to the caller before he spoke again. "Jason, no, don't hang up on me—"

"He hung up?" Julianne asked needlessly as she watched Ben replace the receiver.

"Yep. It's a long story that I really can't tell you, but he'll call back again. One of these days. What were we talking about? The tornado?"

"Yes. Is Betty's house all right?"

"Yes, her home wasn't hit. Most of the damage was in the mobile home park close to the lake. One trailer was completely destroyed." Ben motioned for

Julianne to have a seat in a nearby chair, then he eased into the office chair behind his large oak desk and leaned back. "I've put together some supplies to take over later. They need everything. Food, clothing, linens, water, you name it."

"If you need to go over there, Ben, please, go ahead," Julianne offered and started to stand up. "We can talk another time."

"No," Ben responded and pulled his chair forward, closer to his desk. "I want to talk to you now. I can go back over there later." Ben studied Julianne's pensive expression. "What's going on with you these days? We haven't had much of a chance to talk lately."

Julianne took a deep breath and let it out in an audible sigh. She'd have to admit to the pastor his earlier advice had been on target. The O'Hara family had complicated her life. "Remember that night at the laundromat about a month ago? When we talked about the O'Hara twins?"

Reverend Ben nodded and watched as Julianne's deep-brown eyes filled with tears.

"Well, you were right. They're not like any of the other kids in my class, Ben." Julianne looked down to reach into her skirt pocket for a tissue. "I love them, I mean, really love them," she admitted and raised her gaze to meet his eyes. "And they need a mother."

"And...?" He waited.

"Their father asked me to marry him." She blinked hard. How she wished she could say that Luke O'Hara had fallen madly in love with her and wanted to spend the rest of his life with her. Or that with their first kiss they had realized they were meant to be together, rather than that their first kiss had also been their last. At least, to this point in time. "I think I'm going to accept his offer."

Ben raised a hand to his mouth thoughtfully for a moment. "When did he ask you?"

"Last night."

A knock at the office door drew both Ben and Julianne's attention toward the intrusion. The wooden door slowly eased open, and Emma Fulton poked her head into the room. "There's a phone call for you, Reverend. It's Mrs. Peyton, the woman who lost her mobile home in the tornado...and she's crying."

Julianne wiped her own eyes with the crumpled tissue, and Ben nodded toward his secretary.

"Ask her to hold for a moment, and, Emma, next time, use the intercom, please."

Emma's sheepish look moved from her boss's disgruntled expression to Julianne's solemn face before she shut the door to return to her desk.

"I'm sorry about that," Ben remarked when he glanced apologetically toward Julianne. "I'll talk to Emma later about that interruption."

"Let it go, Ben. She just wants to know why I'm in here."

"And, as much as I like her, it's none of her business why you're in here."

The blinking light on Ben's office phone caught Julianne's eye. "Do you want me to step outside while you take this call?"

"No, that's not necessary. This will only take a minute." Then Ben picked up the receiver and spoke briefly to the distressed Mrs. Peyton on the other end of the line. Julianne stared at the colorful playground equipment through the window of the pastor's office until he concluded his brief conversation.

"She's going to be staying with the older couple who manage the mobile home park," Ben explained after he hung up the receiver. "She has two little boys, ages three and five, who have lost all of their toys and clothes."

"Do you need to go over there?" Julianne asked. "We could talk tomorrow."

"I don't like to cancel out on you like that, Julianne. If you need to talk about this—"

"It will keep," she offered with a smile. "That woman's problems are much bigger than mine at the moment."

Ben drummed his fingers momentarily on his desk. "Mrs. Peyton did seem very upset."

Julianne realized Ben's awkward decision— weighing whether to continue this important discussion with his friend who obviously needed his advice or to go to Mrs. Peyton's aid. She wanted to help tip the scales in the other woman's direction. Talking about her own concerns seemed trivial compared to the real need that existed just a few short miles away. "Why don't we go over to the variety store and ask if they'll donate some clothing for her kids? Then we could stop at the grocery store to pick up a few things. Maybe Emma would want to come with us."

And Emma did choose to join them. She even

asked Reverend Ben to stop off at her husband's hardware store on their way out of Fairweather so they could pick up some tools, flashlights and batteries that Sam was willing to contribute to the cause. Soon Reverend Ben, Julianne and Emma found themselves in Baylor's Landing, looking over the disaster site of twisted metal and belongings that the tornado had caused. They delivered the clothing and toy trucks the variety store had given, the items from Fairweather's hardware store and the sacks of food that they themselves had purchased for the family to help get them through the immediate crisis.

Mrs. Peyton turned out to be a very attractive redhead, Julianne noticed immediately. A woman probably in her late twenties or early thirties, Emma surmised when out of hearing range. And available. There was no Mr. Peyton in the picture, although Emma hadn't gotten to the bottom of the mystery yet to find out why this young, pretty mom was alone in the world. But, Julianne was quite sure, if anyone could get the facts, it would be Emma Fulton.

"She doesn't go to church anywhere, Reverend Ben," Emma was quick to point out on their return trip back to Fairweather. "Hasn't since she was a child, she told me."

Julianne's elbow pressed against the armrest, and she covered her mouth with her hand to hide an unstoppable grin. Reverend Ben gave Julianne a knowing sideways glance as he drove his car toward home with Emma chattering away in the back seat.

"Think she'll be willing to visit The Old First Church?" the pastor asked.

"If you were to ask her, I'm sure she would," Emma remarked. "She ought to, considering all of the help we've given her today."

"But we shouldn't look at it that way, Emma. We're not giving her things to pressure her into coming to our church. We're helping her because she needs help. We're Christians. Helping people is what we do. Remember last week's sermon? Matthew 25: 35-36? 'For I was hungry and you gave me something to eat, I was thirsty and you gave me something to drink, I was a stranger and you invited me in, I needed clothes and you clothed me, I was sick and you looked after me, I was in prison and you came to visit me.'"

"I remember," Julianne remarked. "In verse 40 the Lord replies that whatever you did for one of His brothers, you did for Him."

"True, true," came Emma's reluctant agreement, "but, still..."

Julianne only half listened to the continuing banter between the pastor and his secretary. Her mind was on Luke and the children. She missed them. Mrs. Peyton's little boys had only reminded Julianne of the tomato soup and grilled cheese sandwiches she was missing with Nora and Todd. And Luke. How could she not marry him? He offered everything she wanted, everything except his heart.

The Welcome To Fairweather sign was soon plainly visible as the three of them returned to the community. They were nearing the center when Reverend Ben asked, "Do you want me to take you home, Julianne, or is there a need for you to stop at the center?''

"Home would be fine, Ben. I'll finish up in my classroom in the morning.''

"Thanks for going with us," he offered as they approached the apartment Julianne rented. "And I'm sorry about the interruption of our conversation. Could you meet with me tomorrow afternoon? Maybe your assistant could handle the kids alone for a little while so we could talk?''

"Maybe," Julianne responded. "Or, perhaps, at the end of the day again? That might work best." It would definitely work best, Julianne knew. She had no desire to return to teaching with eyes reddened from crying, and that was a very real possibility if she met with Ben early in the day. What if his advice wasn't the positive one she needed it to be?

"Stop in the office in the morning and check my schedule if you have time," the pastor said. "We'll talk tomorrow. And, again, I'm sorry about today.''

Julianne smiled and climbed out of the car. "That's okay. I feel good about helping the Peytons. Did you see those kids' faces light up when we handed them each a toy truck? For a moment there, in the middle of all that loss and destruction, it seemed like all was right with the world." Reverend Ben nodded with a smile of agreement, then Julianne glanced into the back seat. "Good night, Emma. See you in the morning.''

Julianne turned and slowly mounted the steps. Turning the key in the lock, she walked inside her home, an apartment she had loved. Until recently. It was too quiet. Not even her still-living goldfish could cheer her up tonight. The phone on the wall was the first thing that her gaze fell on when she entered the front door. Calling Luke would be comforting, but to say what? That she was no closer to an answer this night than she had been the night before? That she loved his children, she wanted to love him and— *Oh, Lord, pleeease*—couldn't he love her? Now, completely, forever? Tossing her purse on the coffee table, she sank into the cushions of her sofa. Until the phone rang.

She grabbed up the receiver. "Hello?"

"Hi, Julianne." It was Luke, and he hesitated before continuing. "I just wanted to make sure you got home all right from the center. You usually walk home, and it's getting dark outside." He paused again. "I didn't know how late you'd be staying there with Reverend Hunter."

"We didn't stay there long at all, actually," she answered. "We ended up going over to Baylor's Landing to take some supplies to a family who lost their home today in that tornado. We weren't in his office over five or ten minutes."

"That was good of you, to help that family, I mean. Were they hurt in the storm?"

"No, no, thank the Lord. Physically, they're fine. It's a young woman and her two little boys, and they've lost everything...everything except each other, and, of course, that's the most important thing of all. I guess we need to remember that."

"True," Luke remarked and moved a hand to the back of his neck to rub an aching muscle. "They can always start over again." Just like I want to do, he thought the silent words. With you. "So, then you enjoyed your evening with Reverend Hunter?"

"Enjoy? I guess you could say that. Emma Fulton went with us to Baylor's Landing. I couldn't discuss anything personal with Ben while Emma was present, so I'm going to meet with him again tomorrow."

Luke didn't respond right away. He didn't take this piece of information as good news. It was probably the beginning of more time spent with Reverend Hunter and less with the O'Haras. It might be something he would be forced to accept. "All right," he replied. What else could he say? "Then, maybe, if you're free the next night, you could have dinner with us?"

"Yes, I'd like that," Julianne answered, then caught her lower lip between her teeth until it throbbed. Did she detect a note of jealousy in this man's voice? She hoped so. It offered bright hope for tomorrow. "Luke, I just feel I need to talk to Ben, as my pastor—"

"And as your friend," Luke added.

Yep. He sounded jealous. Julianne smiled. "As my friend, but mostly as my pastor. This is a big decision, Luke. For both of us. Marriage is a huge commitment. I need to believe it's the right thing to do. Talking to Ben might help me."

He cleared his throat. "I understand, Julianne. Talk to whomever you need to talk to about this. Take your time. I don't want you to make a mistake."

"It's not just me I'm concerned about. It could be a mistake for you, too."

No, there'd be no mistake for him, but how could he tell her? How did he even know? Yet, somehow, deep down, he did. Julianne was the woman he needed to heal this ache within. But he wouldn't rush her, he wouldn't push her into this commitment no matter how much he wanted to do exactly those things. He wanted a future with her as his wife, and he wanted to be assured of it soon, before he lost her to a life as a pastor's wife. "I know. We need to do the right thing, for both of us. But…" Did he dare say how he really felt? That he knew deep in his heart that this was the right thing? She was the right woman? This was the right time? "Julianne, I believe that for me and for my children, marrying you is the right thing."

But why? The words practically screamed in her mind. Why couldn't he say what he felt? Was he jealous of Ben Hunter or not? Did Luke feel anything more than friendship for her? And, if not, how could he explain the longing that had pulled them into that kiss not so long ago? Or the joy that filled her heart every time she saw him? "Luke…" she began, then stopped. The children would be enough to keep them together, to make them a family, but she wanted more from Luke O'Hara than he'd offered. Maybe that was her mistake. "I want to believe it's the right thing. Just give me time to be sure. I need to be sure."

"I know you do," Luke agreed. "I want that for you, too. Honestly." He was silent for a moment.

The house was still. Both children were sleeping. And Luke felt like he held their future in his hands. But it was Julianne's future, too. "If you think...if you come to the conclusion that this won't work for you... Julianne, what I'm trying to say is that...if you feel drawn to Ben Hunter, I would understand."

He would understand. How would he understand when she wouldn't? Unless, he was giving her an easy way out. Had he had a change of heart about the proposal? "Luke, Ben Hunter is my pastor, my friend. I have no romantic notions about him. That's not an issue with us."

"All right, then. I'll see you in the morning, when I drop off the kids. About seven-thirty."

"Okay, I'll see you then." But Julianne didn't want to say goodbye yet. "Did Nora and Todd have a good evening?"

"Yes, they did," Luke answered. "We visited Maggie for a little while. She won't be back to the center. She's just too exhausted to work right now."

"She should stay home, stay off her feet. They've waited so long to have this baby. I hope Frank insists she takes it easy."

"He will. He's more worried about her than you and I are. I think, if he could afford to close the Book-Stop and stay home to take care of her for the next couple of months, he would do exactly that," Luke remarked.

"You're right. He adores Maggie. It shows in practically everything he does." Julianne closed her eyes, her heart suddenly aching. She wanted a marriage like that, a husband like that. And she wanted

Luke O'Hara. Could she have all of that together? Was it right there for the taking?

Luke quietly agreed with her. "Frank Wren is a good husband, probably the best I've seen. I think it will all work out for them. At least, I want to think that."

"Me, too." Julianne sighed softly. "I keep praying that it will although it's difficult to pray for God's will to be done in a case like this. I keep asking for a healthy little baby for them. I want what Maggie wants."

"You'll have that someday, Julianne," Luke stated quietly.

"No, I don't mean for me. I mean, for Maggie. I want her to have a baby of her own to love." Then Julianne considered telling Luke what she'd not mentioned before. That she would most likely never have what Maggie has at this moment—a healthy child flourishing inside of her. "Luke…" Wouldn't her revelation only put added pressure on him to go through with the marriage even if he changed his mind, so as not to deny her raising the twins she'd fallen in love with? She didn't want a wedding based on a sense of obligation. That would never stand the test of time. "I'm kind of tired. I guess I'll see you and the kids in the morning," she offered, trying to bring the conversation to an end before she told more than she should. "Thanks for calling me."

"I'm glad I called," he admitted. "I wanted to know you were home safely."

"And I am. Have a good night's sleep, Luke. I'll talk to you tomorrow."

They both hung up their phones and sat down, alone on their living room sofas. There wasn't much chance either one of them would get the good night's sleep they needed.

This had followed a request she made of the Peytons the night before. They had told her about each other, saying good-bye and goodnight in sign language.

Chapter Eight

"Can't you use some of the church offering money to buy them what they need?" Julianne asked Reverend Ben when she saw him standing by Emma Fulton's desk early the next day. She had just overheard him discussing some additional needs of the Peytons with his secretary and lamenting the lack of funds to supply the same.

Reverend Ben turned to see Julianne standing in the doorway. "Not without getting approval from the majority of the board members. Do you want a doughnut? Emma made them." He pointed toward a nearby plate.

"Made them?" Julianne looked toward Emma. "I didn't know there was such a thing as homemade doughnuts."

Emma smiled broadly. "Sam just loves them. He thinks they're tastier than any he's ever eaten from a bakery, so every now and then I surprise him with a fresh batch. This morning, I decided to make extras to bring to work.''

Reverend Ben took a drink from the coffee cup he held in his hand. "They're delicious, Julianne. Really. Try one.''

So she did reach for one, and Reverend Ben was right. It was scrumptious. Julianne thanked Emma for the delicious breakfast before attempting to recall what she'd been talking about.

"The board members,'' she remembered aloud. "Why don't you call them? There's not one of them that would oppose this project of helping a tornado victim with young children. How could they? 'Except for the grace of God, there go I' as the saying implies. That could be one of them out there—homeless and hungry.''

"Not everyone is as quick to approve of my projects as you are, Julianne.'' Ben's smile had a sad slant to it. He sat his coffee down on Emma's desk. "I wish they were.''

"But you're well liked and respected, Ben. I think you have come a long way from the disgruntled attitudes of the members when you first started here three years ago. The days of living in the shadow of Reverend Olsen are over.''

"Those days will never be over, Julianne. Not totally,'' Ben replied. "It's not that simple.''

"But if you explain the seriousness of this need and the urgency of it, the board members will agree with you. Don't you think so, Emma?'' Julianne had defended Ben Hunter from the moment he'd arrived in town. Sometimes old ways needed to pass away and new ways had to be accepted. And Emma Fulton had been one of the slower ones to come around to the young pastor's way of thinking.

"Yes, Reverend Ben. I do think they'd agree with you. Mrs. Peyton is a legitimate case of need, worthy, I think, of all the help we can give her." Then one of Emma's eyebrows raised in apparent warning. "Help in the financial way, I mean, of course. I think letting this young woman bend your ear or cry on your shoulder a bit too much wouldn't be a good thing. She's far too pretty and too available for you to allow any encouragement. It might lead to a wrong way of thinking for someone."

"For whom?" Julianne asked in disbelief. Had she understood Emma Fulton's implication correctly?

"For Mrs. Peyton. The board members. The community."

"Emma?" Julianne rose to Ben's defense immediately. And with gusto. "How could you imply such a thing? Ben's never done anything questionable. Just because this tornado victim happens to be young, pretty and single doesn't mean she could be Ben's downfall. Real or imagined."

Emma was quick to respond. "I'm not saying he's interested in her, Julianne. I'm saying that appearances are important. Just as I was here last night when Reverend Ben met with you in his office, he needs to be equally as cautious—maybe even more so—in this situation. People can very easily get the wrong impression about things like that." Emma pulled her cardigan tightly around herself as her face flushed with color. "It would be wise for all of us to keep that in mind."

Julianne suddenly felt that she, too, was being warned, but about what, she couldn't be certain. Was she spending too much time alone with Luke and the children? Were people talking? And, if so, what were they saying? That there was something wrong with the relationship? But before she could respond with her questions, Reverend Ben wisely intervened.

"Unfortunately, Emma is right, Julianne. The nature of people tends to be to think the worst. Emma, perhaps you could come along again the next time I go to Baylor's Landing. I'm sure that with you present, there would be less speculation about the situation. I have no interest in being misunderstood by anyone. Including Mrs. Peyton."

"Very well, then," Emma answered quickly, in a tense reply. "I'm always glad to help out when you need me."

"Emma—" Julianne started to speak, but Ben immediately cut off her words.

"Could I talk to you for a moment?" he asked, then gingerly cupped her elbow in his hand and steered her away from Emma Fulton's desk into the solitude of his office. Then the door closed behind them. "Please, Julianne, don't argue with her. She means well."

"But did you hear what she was saying? About you? And, I think, maybe, about me? We're adults, Ben. If we choose to spend time with someone, whatever the reason, it's our business. Not Emma Fulton's." Eyeing a small trash can, Julianne approached it and in went the remainder of her doughnut. It had rather suddenly lost its taste.

"But we are trying to set good examples, aren't we, Julianne?"

"Yes, but—"

"Sometimes we need to listen, whether we want to or not. Sometimes it's not pleasant."

Julianne crossed her arms in front of her as she watched Ben take a seat and rub a hand across his forehead. "Boy, do I have a headache," he remarked.

"And you'll continue to have them as long as you allow other people to dictate your behavior for you." Julianne sat down in the nearest chair.

"It's not other people who dictate my behavior to me, Julianne. It's God. And if I occasionally hear His wisdom in the words of others, I try to listen— whether I like it or not."

"And am I supposed to listen, too? Don't you think there was an inference to me in what Emma was saying? That I should watch what I do? Is my spending time with Luke and the children in some way misconstrued by others? I'm a grown woman, Ben. If I choose to be with Luke O'Hara, in a way that is proper and acceptable in God's eyes, then that's exactly what I'm going to do—no matter what Emma Fulton or anyone else says about it."

"Okay, let's talk about you and Luke O'Hara. How complicated is this, Julianne? Do you love him?" Ben asked, blunt and to the point.

Julianne sat up a little straighter in her chair. "I

don't think so. I mean, I think I could, but it really hasn't been that kind of a relationship…yet."

"So, it's an arrangement then? One to benefit Luke O'Hara, mostly?"

"I wouldn't say that exactly, either," Julianne defended. "It would benefit me, too. I mean, Ben, you know, I can't have a baby. But with Nora and Todd—"

"With Nora and Todd, you'd be an instant mother," Ben agreed quietly. "But you're going to become someone's wife, too, Julianne. Marriage is a very serious step. You and Luke should come in for counseling."

"I don't know that Luke would agree to that," Julianne replied. Premarital counseling? She hadn't even considered such a thing. She'd thought this would be easy. Just get a license, recruit Reverend Ben and say I do. "Ben, this would be much different from one of your usual weddings. We're not kids. Couldn't we dispense with the counseling and—"

"And go right to the altar? I don't think so, Julianne. This wedding may not mean much to you or Luke in its beginning, but it would still be a commitment to be honored in the eyes of God. A marriage can't be taken lightly."

"I'm not taking it lightly. It would mean something to both of us." She paused. At least, it would mean something to her. Maybe she couldn't really speak for Luke. "Are you totally against marriages of convenience?"

"Not at all," Ben remarked. "I've seen several that have really worked out well. But in every case, both of the parties were Christians, Julianne. They went into the relationship with a lifetime commitment. It wasn't a quick fix that could be undone later.''

Julianne's heartbeat quickened in dread. She hadn't considered that possibility. "But this wouldn't be that way, either. Luke is too careful, thoughtful, too kind to do something like that to me or the kids. He...I...we care for each other, very much. It just doesn't happen to be the romantic beginning most couples start out with.''

"But it should be," Ben remarked in quiet opposition. "You deserve that kind of happiness, Julianne. Don't sacrifice it for the needs of the O'Hara children. Or their father.''

"Don't look at it that way, Ben," Julianne was nearly at a loss for words. This morning certainly was starting out all wrong. "This marriage to Luke is what I want.''

Reverend Ben was silent far too long to suit Julianne. He looked away from her questioning eyes toward the brown leather Bible on the corner of his desk.

Julianne's nerves tensed into a knot that gripped her stomach. "Ben, can't you see that maybe the Lord is working in this situation? I could be a mother to two little children who need me, and they could be the children I was hoping to have as my own. This marriage could be an answer to my prayers.'' She stirred uneasily in the chair.

"Julianne, if Luke was still a Christian, I might agree with you. But he's not. Maggie has told me about Luke losing his faith in the Lord. He rarely attends church, and when he does, I think it's mainly in deference to Maggie's persistent requests.''

"But he wants his children raised as Christians, Ben.''

"Because he promised his first wife that he would do so. It's through no real desire of his own.'' Ben returned his gaze to study Julianne's crestfallen expression. "I don't want to hurt you, but I must tell you what I honestly think. The Scriptures clearly teach that we are 'not to be yoked together with unbelievers.' You're a Christian, Luke isn't. 'What fellowship can light have with darkness?' I preach that, I live that...I believe that to be true.''

"But Luke will come around, given enough time. I know he will love the Lord again someday.'' The words rushed from Julianne as the color drained from her face. "I can get him to come to church with us— as a family. I'm—I'm almost sure of it.''

"'Almost' isn't good enough. You can't marry someone with the idea that you're going to change a very basic and fundamental belief that they hold to. Luke has every right not to serve the Lord if he doesn't want to. In fact, ironically, it's his God-given right. The Lord gives us a free will to do as we wish, and Luke has chosen to not believe any longer. He might never believe in God again, Julianne. And where do you fit into that picture?''

"But there's Nora and Todd to consider, too. They need a Christian mother. They need to be in Sunday school and church regularly. I can do that for them. I could be the reason they grow up loving the Lord.''

"Maybe," Ben agreed with visible reluctance. He leaned back in his chair and rubbed a hand down his face in frustration. "But what if things go badly? What if you feel that you have to walk away from God, too, to join your husband in his disbelief?"

"Ben, I would never—"

"We can't say what we'd never do, because we don't know for certain how we will react to a given set of circumstances." Ben pulled his chair closer to his desk and leaned forward slightly as if to emphasize the gravity of his words. "You're a Christian, Julianne. You've given your heart to the Lord. You've placed your life in His hands, wanting His will to be done. You've testified to it, you've lived it. Don't abandon it."

Julianne shifted nervously in her seat, growing increasingly uncomfortable with the truth in her pastor's words. "I wouldn't be abandoning anything."

"Don't let your feelings for these children, or this man, pull you down spiritually. If you don't love Luke now, maybe someday you will. Truly, deeply love him. Then what will you do if the years go by, and he refuses to open his heart to God? I'm sorry I have to say this to you, but—"

"I don't want to hear any more," she said rather than listen with rising dismay. "I came here hoping to hear helpful advice from my pastor."

"And I'm giving that to you. But that's the role I play in your life right now. A pastor. I can't be just your friend in this moment, Julianne, and tell you what you want to hear. It's the pastor in me that is speaking. It has to be. That's what God expects of me."

"All right," she relented before standing up. Her eyes clouded with tears as she turned to leave. "You've been honest with your feelings. That's all I can ask from you."

"Don't go away crying. Sit down, Julianne. Your assistant can handle the class for a while without you. She's done that before," Ben insisted. "Let me call Betty to tell her you've been delayed, and she can go up to check on the kids." He picked up the phone.

"No, thank you," Julianne replied, clasping her slender hands together and staring at them rather than meeting her pastor's eyes. "I'll be fine. Really. I'll stop at the rest room on my way back to class to wipe up my mascara." She stole a quick glance at Ben. It had hurt him to be so frank with her. She could see that in his sad expression. "If I do marry Luke, you won't perform the ceremony?"

He shook his head, slowly. "I'm sorry, Julianne, but it's not something I can do."

She sniffed and nodded her head. His answer hadn't surprised her, but she needed to know. "I should get back to my class," she said hastily, wanting out of Ben's presence. Reaching for the doorknob, she started to exit.

"Julianne..."

She looked back toward him, dreading the final words on the subject.

"I'll attend the ceremony, if you can forgive me enough to invite me."

"And why would you want to come?" Julianne asked.

"Because I wouldn't want to miss the wedding of a good friend—even if it's a match I don't entirely approve of."

Julianne gave a small smile through her tears, then she turned to go. She was glad to get away from Reverend Ben and his hard words. Emma was not at her desk, much to Julianne's relief, when she made her way silently through the office area toward the ladies' rest room. Pushing open the heavy door, she stepped inside and surveyed the damage to her makeup in the wide mirror. She pulled some toilet paper from a roll and wiped away the smudges. Just what did she see in those dark eyes that looked back at her? Caution, maybe? Insecurity, uneasiness, uncertainty—definitely. Was Reverend Ben's word definitive on the matter of her marriage to Luke? Had she decided that whatever her pastor said, she would do? No. She hadn't decided that at all, she reminded herself. In fact, she would find her own answer. And the answer was probably waiting for her back with the four-year-old group, in two pairs of blue eyes that would light up the moment Julianne entered the classroom. How could she walk away from that?

Chapter Nine

"**I**'m glad you could come for dinner tonight," Luke remarked to Julianne when they entered the living room of his house to relax after their meal. The four of them had enjoyed a variety of items Luke had picked up from Olaf's Deli on the way home from work he'd done over in Baylor's Landing that day. When he picked up the children at the center, they'd asked Julianne to eat with them. She'd agreed to join them, and the children were elated. Luke, on the other hand, was relieved. Maybe her appointments with Reverend Hunter were really over. He certainly hoped so. A future with Julianne was what Luke wanted, it was what the children needed. He hoped she'd see it that way, too, although at this point he wasn't sure which way it might go. But his many concerns were about to be resolved by his inquisitive and impatient young daughter.

"Will you be my new mommy?" Nora's whis-

pered question brought instant tears to Julianne's
eyes. She hugged the little girl who had crawled up
onto her lap.

"Oh, sweetie, I'd love to," Julianne admitted, allowing her heart to make the decision her head could
not make. A deep calmness settled over her. She'd
chosen the direction she would take, and it would be
with these children. And Luke. She raised her eyes
to see him standing beside the large window in the
living room, staring at the sunset. He turned to look
at her, studying her for the moment. She smiled. Had
he heard her words, she wondered.

"Is that a yes?" he asked quietly as his brows knit
into a doubtful expression.

"Yes, Luke. I'll marry you," Julianne could
hardly believe she was saying the words. She'd prac-
ticed both ways. Yes and no, considering how it
might feel to say one or the other. But the *yes* felt
much better than she had thought it might, regardless
of Reverend Ben's negative perspective. It seemed
right, for some undefinable reason, and even more so
when Luke's face brightened with a wide grin.

"You're sure? Absolutely sure, Julianne?"

"Yes," she replied and let a soft sigh escape.
"I've thought about it long enough. I want to be part
of this family."

The immediate hurrays of the twins filled the room
with lots of happy noise. Nora was up off Julianne's
lap, giving her a huge wet kiss and then rushing off
to dance around in circles with Todd, who had overheard the conversation from the corner of the room
where he was playing with his fire engine.

Luke glanced at his excited kids and then walked over to where Julianne was seated on the sofa. She smiled up at him as he reached to take her hand in his and pull her to her feet. "Thank you," he said. The clear blue gaze that remained transfixed on Julianne's face revealed more than his words did. They were filled with a blessed mix of gratitude, hope and a look she could only read as *I can't believe I'm this lucky,* which ended Julianne's concerns about whether Luke wanted her for his wife. He did. Luke leaned forward and tenderly kissed her temple. "Thank you, Julianne."

"Thank you for trusting me with your children," she answered with an unsteady smile. "I love them, Luke."

"I know," he replied and kissed her on the temple again, his warm mouth lingering there a moment longer than necessary.

A better kiss would have been in order under normal circumstances, but then this marriage proposal hadn't been offered in the usual way, Julianne reminded herself. Luke released her hand and picked up Todd who had come running to his father.

"Is she going to live with us?" Todd asked with a broad grin.

"Yes, she is," Luke said, resisting an urge to look into Julianne's dark eyes again.

"Starting now?" Nora's question came from across the room where she was jumping up and down and clapping her little hands. "Tonight?"

"No, but soon," Luke replied.

"When?"

"When?" he repeated the question, as he tilted his head to the side enough to see Julianne's uncertain shrug.

"When did you have in mind?" she asked.

"Yesterday," he stated and smiled.

She laughed softly. That sounded good to her, too. Then a lot of the uncertainties would be behind her.

"How about next Saturday?" was his counteroffer. "We could get your things moved in here by then."

Her hand flew to her mouth. "I forgot about my rental agreement on my apartment. I'll lose my security deposit if I move without giving the landlord a reasonable notice."

"Let him keep it."

"But, Luke, it was three hundred dollars. I can't afford—"

"I can," Luke remarked before setting Todd on the floor. "I'll take care of it." He glanced back at her, suddenly realizing he should probably see if she had any objections. "Okay?"

"Okay," she answered. "If you're sure."

"I'm sure," he told her. "Come upstairs and I'll show you my office."

Julianne and the twins followed him upstairs where the kids took off for their own bedroom to play while Julianne entered the office Luke had referred to.

"I'll move the computer into my room along with these filing cabinets." He slid open a wide closet that was empty except for some shoes in the bottom. Luke glanced at the denim jumper over the white cotton shirt she wore. She seemed to own a lot of different outfits. "Will this be enough space for your clothes?"

"Yes, that will be fine," she answered before looking around the room. The wallpaper was ivory with a small flower print in white. The curtains, ivory with ruffles along the bottom, must have been a choice of Maggie's. "This room is pretty. The carpet is the color of—"

"Cocoa," Luke finished her sentence. "My sister loves this carpeting. She picked it out."

"It's lovely." So this would be her room here in Luke's house. How strange this change was going to feel. Living here, sleeping here. The nagging in the back of her mind returned. Was this the right decision? Could she be Luke's wife? Like this? With a room of her own and his children to raise? Would loving them be enough?

Her doubts must have shown in her eyes as Luke regarded her quizzically for a moment. "Julianne, if you're not sure about this…"

"I'm sure," she stated and slid her hands into the pockets of her jumper. Absolutely, positively, almost sure, she mused. But she did know she loved the twins. In regard to their father… She studied Luke's profile as he walked to the window to adjust the air conditioner. She very much liked what she knew of him. Reverend Ben was wrong, she'd told herself dozens of times. Luke O'Hara would trust the Lord again. She'd find a way to help him recover the faith he'd lost. She had to. Her whole future, as well as the kids', depended upon it.

"This house is old, and it doesn't have central air. These window units will have to do until I get that taken care of."

"I'm used to it," she remarked. "I have window units in my apartment."

"I'll see if I can hire Travis, Mark or Mike to help me with the moving."

"Who are they?"

"The college guys who have been helping me with the landscaping jobs in Minneapolis. Frank knew them and lined them up to work with me over the summer. Anyway, maybe one of them would like to make some extra money in the evenings this week."

"We'll definitely need help, Luke. That stairway will be very hard to bring furniture down. Two of my brothers helped me move in. They told me I'd have to live there the rest of my life because there was no way on earth they were going to haul that furniture back down the stairs. It had been horrible enough getting it up there."

"We'll get it taken care of, one way or another," Luke said with a grin. "And, don't worry, I won't call your brothers." He hesitated. "You've not said much about your family. Doesn't one of your brothers live in Minneapolis?"

"Yes, one does. The rest of my siblings are scattered around the country. There were six of us, three boys, three girls."

"Six?" Luke remarked. "Big family. No wonder you're so good with kids. You've probably been around them most of your life."

"Yes," she agreed, "I have."

"Julianne, if someday...when you're ready," Luke stammered, "if you want to have other children..."

She raised her gaze to meet his. Here was the subject she'd been avoiding, coming right at her. Ready or not. She looked away. "No, we can't, Luke. I mean, I can't. At least, if my doctor knows what she's talking about, I can't."

Luke's frown was slight, as though he were trying to understand. "You can't? Are you sure?"

"Well, I haven't tried, if that's what you mean," she remarked quietly. "Craig and I were engaged, not married."

"No, no, that's not what I mean at all, Julianne. I—I just can't think that at your young age, it could be a certainty. Did your doctor do tests? Does she have real reason to think that you can't have a baby?"

"I had a regular examination, but she found a problem that was significant enough to pretty much rule out pregnancy for me. I have something called endometriosis. Often, laser surgery can correct the problem enough to allow for conception, but Dr. Franklin believes that my case is serious enough that surgery wouldn't help significantly." She folded her hands together nervously and swallowed hard. "So, if you want more children, Luke, then you don't want me."

"Don't say that," he objected. He reached out, cupping her chin tenderly in his hand. "It's you I want, Julianne, not more children. I want the family that I already have to be whole again, nor-mal...happy. You offer us all of those things—and more.''

"Luke, I don't know if I can live up to all that you think I can do, but I'll try. Hopefully, with the Lord's help, it will be enough.''

"It will be more than enough, but I'm sorry you can never have a baby, Julianne,'' he answered, and his arms instinctively encircled her in a comforting embrace. "I can only imagine how much that hurts. But I want you to know that you are exactly who we need in our lives. You. Only you.''

She nodded, her cheek rubbing against the soft fabric of his shirt. She hoped he was right. It would have been nice to think that at least one of them was certain they knew what they were getting themselves into with this marriage of convenience.

"I'll—I'll say good night to the kids, then I need to go home,'' she said when Luke slowly released her. She wondered if he felt as awkward about the moment as she did, but glancing at his sober expres-sion gave her no clue. "I have things to do, things to pack if we're really getting married so soon.''

"Don't go,'' he said quickly. "I want to talk for a few minutes more, if you don't mind.''

"I don't mind,'' she agreed and waited.

"Julianne, listen to me,'' he said quietly, tenderly. His hands sank into the pockets of his slacks as he stood searching her eyes for clear understanding of the relationship they were about to embark on. "I very much want you to be my wife. Nora and Todd are all the children I need in this lifetime. They make me happy, they fulfill that desire in me to be a parent, and I want to share them with you. They need you, desperately, but if you never have a baby of your own... All I'm trying to ask is, do you think the twins will be enough for you? Enough to satisfy you in the years to come?''

"But don't you see?'' she asked softly. "I need them, too, Luke. They'll be all I have. They're the only children that can make me a parent. But if you marry me, can you be sure you won't change your mind later? Want someone different, someone you can have another child with?'' A heavy sadness gripped her heart at the thought.

His smile seemed bittersweet. "No, Julianne, I didn't want to marry again. Ever. That was my original intention when I started out alone with the kids, and the only reason I've changed my mind is because of you—your love for the kids, their love for you.'' Luke reached out and took one of her hands in his own. "I know it's not the romantic beginning to a relationship that you deserve.''

"Luke, I don't care.''

"But you should care. You are a beautiful, wonderful young woman who is entitled to a lot more than you're getting with me. That's why I need you to think carefully about your friendship with Reverend Hunter.''

Julianne gave him a quizzical look. "Ben? Why?''

Luke hesitated. "Are you certain that a marriage between you and the pastor is not a possibility?''

"Ben and me? Why? What difference—''

"The difference being, he can offer you a better life than I can."

Her eyes widened in surprise. "What makes you think that? I'm not in love with him."

"You're not in love with me, either, but you're willing to marry me. Think about it, Julianne. You marry me, you live with the past. Daily. You'll have another woman's children to raise. With Ben you wouldn't have that burden to face. I had thought— until tonight—that you could have a child of your own with a husband you love. I didn't want to take that away from you."

"Ben and I have no romantic feelings for each other. We never did. There's no chemistry, no attraction like that between us. Nothing."

Luke looked down at her hand momentarily, and Julianne wondered if he felt as she did. Chemistry wasn't going to be a problem for them—at least, not from her point of view.

"So, the wedding's on?" Luke asked with a smile of obvious relief when he glanced back into her tender gaze.

"As long as you want it to be."

"I do. What about your parents? You'll want them there. And your brothers and sisters?"

"No, I don't want to do it that way. It can be just us. And Maggie and Frank."

Luke studied the determination in her dark eyes. "You'll regret that decision. Trust me on this—at least your mother and father should be there."

"No. I've already decided how I want to do this. My family was far too involved in my wedding plans with Craig Johnson. Then, to all of their shock and disappointment, we called it off. I want to do this quickly, with just us—a simple ceremony and we're married.''

But Luke looked skeptical. ''I feel like I'm taking enough away from you without eliminating a real wedding, too.''

''No. No big wedding. Just us. That's the way I want it. Please, Luke. And the sooner the better.''

The last part Luke didn't argue with. ''I'd marry you, here and now, if it could be arranged.''

But the earliest date they could come up with was Saturday, and Julianne, they agreed, would start moving things into her room at the O'Hara house the next day.

When she left Luke and the kids that evening, she'd hugged both children a little longer than necessary. But no one complained. Then Luke reached for her hand, walking to the car with her in comfortable silence. He opened the door so she could slide into the driver's seat. Then he let go of her hand, slowly.

''Good night,'' she said quietly and gave a small smile through the shadows of nightfall. Their relationship, so far, had known few romantic overtones, she realized, and it would take time to develop that aspect of this marriage of convenience. They both had acknowledged that fact. So why was Luke standing there, looking at her with affection evident in his eyes, affection for her she'd not seen before tonight? And why this frantic pounding within her breast? Now?

Then Luke leaned into the car and brushed a kiss, light and tender as the warm evening breeze, against her lips, and Julianne's heart ached with longing for something more than she understood. She didn't love him. Not yet. Did she? And, if not, how could he send her pulse skittering like this with the slightest touch? Craig Johnson had never made her feel like this. No one had.

"Good night, Julianne. Call me when you get home." He spoke quiet words before closing her door securely.

She assured him she would call; then she drove away. On the drive home, Julianne reminded herself, repeatedly, if things didn't turn out the way she hoped they would with Luke, she would still be getting the family she always wanted—two wonderful children to call her own. If that was all she gained, it would be enough to satisfy her through the years. It would be enough. Wouldn't it?

The week literally flew by in Julianne's estimation. Most of her belongings were moved in by Thursday and she was trying to organize her room and watch the children at the same time, after working all day at the day care. By the kids' bedtime of eight o'clock, she was practically ready to fall asleep herself. She would help Luke tuck them in, give them a kiss and then head back to her apartment to finish up what needed to be done there. Friday went by in a similar blur and before she could believe it, Saturday morning dawned.

"Julianne, this dress is wonderful," Maggie remarked. "You look absolutely beautiful in it. Of course," she added with a sigh of feigned disgust, "you'd look beautiful in a grocery bag."

"I have no plans to be seen in one of those soon," Julianne replied. She adjusted her pearl earrings as she stared into the mirror in Maggie's bedroom, where they were preparing for the wedding.

"Luke looks good, too, you know. Have you seen him this morning?"

Julianne smiled. She'd seen him, and Maggie was right. "That black suit is certainly appealing on him. When you said you had a handsome brother, you definitely weren't exaggerating."

"Thanks a lot," Maggie quipped. "You say that as though I've exaggerated lots of things."

Then Julianne grew serious. "Just be certain you're accurate now, Maggie. You're sure Luke wants to go through with this, aren't you? If he had any second thoughts, wouldn't he tell you about them?"

Maggie shrugged her shoulders. "He probably would, but don't worry. He's lucky he found you and he knows it. You're a godsend for my brother and his kids. And a gorgeous one, too. Now, all that's needed is for you and your new husband to fall in love and live happily ever after."

The smile that curved Julianne's faintly pink mouth had a downward curve to one corner of it. Sadness, Maggie knew. She recognized it clearly. "Do you love him, Julianne?"

"I don't know," she answered as truthfully as she knew how. "I feel differently about Luke than I did about Craig. This is deeper, scarier. It feels more grown-up than any other feeling I've had for anyone."

Maggie's face brightened. "Then this relationship must have potential to it. But go slowly. Luke won't rush you into anything. He's not like that."

"I know he's not. He's never been anything but a gentleman to me, Maggie. When Craig Johnson and I were engaged, it was a constant battle. He always wanted more than I was willing to give. But with Luke...what if he doesn't want me...I mean, as his wife. A real wife."

Maggie's laugh was soft but generous. "Honey, you are one of the prettiest women I know. Luke isn't blind to that fact, believe me. He's a man."

"But I'm not talking about something that develops because we both live under the same roof or because it would be 'convenient' for us. I want more than that."

"Whatever you and Luke have together will be far more than convenient—someday—when the time is right. Just be patient. Let things happen naturally. You'll be married to him, you know, Julianne. It's not like there will be rules you need to follow. Take it one day at a time." Maggie grinned. "Or one night at a time, I should say. And remember, with four-year-old twins in the house, there won't be much of anything happening between you and Luke most of the time. But, of course, you'll both be too tired to care."

"You're probably right. Anyway, I'm so grateful to the Lord for Nora and Todd," Julianne said, giving Maggie's arm a reassuring squeeze. "They are what this marriage is about, and they'll be enough for me, Maggie." They had to be, Julianne knew. She'd already made that decision. Adjusting the ribbon ties of her white lace-trimmed jacket in the mirror, she glanced back at Maggie. "How do I look?"

"Beautiful. Rosebud trim and all. I told you that was the perfect dress." Maggie's encouragement was all Julianne needed.

"I think I'm ready to go. Is the minister downstairs yet?"

"Yes, she's here."

"She? You didn't tell me that Frank's cousin was a woman."

"Does it make a difference?" Maggie asked. "She can marry you off just as legally as Reverend Ben could do."

"But won't do," Julianne said. "I know Ben has his reasons, but it still disappointed me that he wouldn't agree to marry us."

"Oh, honey, don't take it so hard. Reverend Ben is obligated as your pastor to advise you, show you all sides of the issue. It doesn't mean you have to live by what he says."

"But he's probably right, you know."

"Well, you're standing here in a wedding dress, ready to join Luke in my living room and commit your life to him in marriage. You're in pretty deep to be getting cold feet now, but if you're having doubts, I'll tell Luke."

"No," Julianne stopped Maggie with a light touch

to her shoulder. "I want to go through with this. I love Nora and Todd. I don't want to lose them."

"Then, let's go. You're a beautiful bride and your groom is waiting." Maggie walked slowly into her own living room with Julianne where only a handful of people were gathered. Nora and Todd were dressed in their best church clothes and standing with their father, watching for Julianne with wide eyes and mouths opened in happy surprise when she finally appeared. Reverend Ben was off to one side as an observer close to where Frank, the best man, was waiting. Maggie with her wide belly evident beneath her yellow maternity dress took her place next to Julianne as matron of honor.

"You should be lying down," Frank whispered to Maggie before the minister could begin the ceremony.

"Quiet. There's a wedding going on," she silenced Frank with a warning frown. "I won't be standing for long." Then Maggie reached for a large bouquet of flowers from the coffee table and handed them to Julianne. Bunches of daisies tied together with white and yellow ribbons were the perfect complement to the bride's dress, just as Maggie had said they would be. Julianne thanked her friend. Then with her hands trembling slightly, she took her place next to Luke, and met his admiring gaze.

"You look beautiful," he leaned over and whispered to his nervous bride.

"Thank you," she responded in a soft voice. "The children look adorable. Did Maggie help with them?"

"Frank did, if you can believe that." He smiled and reached for her hand. "We'll be okay, Julianne. Don't be nervous."

"Aren't you?" she asked, her eyes wide with incredulity.

"Terrified," he admitted. "Ministers have a way of doing that to me."

She wished she could blame her fears on one specific thing, but she couldn't. She was just plain scared. Of everything. Marriage, life as a wife and mother, a lifetime commitment to someone she'd known such a short time. But when she looked up into the eyes of this man who stood next to her, he didn't seem like a stranger at all. It was Luke, the same man she'd become friends with over these past several weeks. No surprises, no frightening unknown. Just a future with Luke and two children she loved.

"Is she our mommy yet?" Nora asked, impatience narrowing her pretty blue eyes.

"I don't think so," Todd answered his sister. "First that preacher has to talk."

Luke and Julianne smiled simultaneously at the kids' not-so-quiet discussion, and the ceremony began.

The words were brief and the promises were enormous, but when they looked into each other's eyes as they repeated the vows, each believed the other would try to live up to the words they'd repeated. When it came time to kiss the bride, Luke paused, studying Julianne's lovely brown eyes a moment before he gave her a gentle kiss that officially sealed their commitment. Julianne exhaled for what she felt may have been the first time since the minister started speaking. A flash of humor brightened Luke's eyes as he gave her hand a tug. "Time to cut the cake," he said with an easy smile. "We have two antsy kids here who need a little more sugar in their systems."

Then the twins, who had been quite good while observing their first wedding, rushed to Julianne, and she knelt down to kiss them both. Nora and Todd hugged her so hard, she dropped the daisies, which Luke quickly retrieved and then suggested to the kids that was enough hugs for the moment. Aunt Maggie and Uncle Frank had a lovely white cake with yellow daisy decorations in the icing, and the children were soon eating small slices that Frank had prepared for them. While Julianne and Luke drank punch and spoke with Ben, Maggie and the visiting pastor who'd just married them.

Married. Julianne let the word sink in. She was Mrs. Luke O'Hara now, for better or for worse. She glanced over at her new husband where he knelt beside Todd instructing him about something. Luke had planned a day of activities for the children today after getting Julianne's okay on the idea. Nora and Todd were what brought this marriage to pass so why not celebrate the occasion with them? At an amusement park, the zoo...whatever Luke had decided on was fine with Julianne. What they did that day didn't matter to her as long as they were together as a family— the family she thought she'd never have.

* * *

"What a day!" Julianne exclaimed as she settled down on the couch in Luke's living room—she corrected her thinking, in *their* living room—with a glass of iced tea in her hand. She slipped off her tennis shoes and slid them under the coffee table. Then she looked over at Luke. "Do you care if I put my feet up on the sofa?"

"No, I don't mind," he stated with a shake of his head, "and you don't have to ask. It's your sofa, too."

"Nope," she differed quickly, her eyes dancing with amusement. "Mine is stored in your garage, if you will recall, and I really don't want to go out there to sit."

"And I don't want you out there," he countered with an easy smile. "You're my wife, Julianne. As of today, my home is your home. In every way."

"Thank you," she said softly as though she accepted the fact, but she knew in her heart that this would take some getting used to. "I'm exhausted," she added before placing her drink on a nearby coaster.

"That could have something to do with the marathon of children's activities we endured today," Luke remarked. He relaxed into a nearby recliner. "The kids never seem to run out of enthusiasm," he added. "I don't know how it is with you at the day care, working with them all day, but up until now you were able to leave at six and get ready for the next day. As a parent, there's no rest period like that in between days."

"Oh, I'll get used to it," Julianne answered.

"That's the kind of problem I guess I've always wanted to have. What do you think they liked better? The kiddy roller coaster or the antique automobiles they helped drive?"

"Hmm," Luke said thoughtfully as he leaned his head back and closed his eyes. "Nora would probably say the roller coaster, and Todd would choose the Model T's, don't you think?"

"Yes," she agreed while letting her gaze linger on the man she had married today. His dark brown hair looked soft and straight, much like his son's. What was it she'd intended to say next? Then she remembered. "Nora definitely liked the bumper cars more than Todd did."

"Their personalities really come out when they get behind the wheel. I'm grateful that Todd is as good-natured as he is."

"I know," Julianne added with a soft laugh. "Nora bumped him relentlessly, and he didn't get angry with her once!"

"He lets her get away with too much," Luke commented. "If Maggie had done that to me when we were kids, I probably would have punched her in the nose first chance I got."

Luke opened his eyes, and Julianne, hoping not to be caught staring, glanced away quickly. She averted her gaze to the front window before commenting, "I can almost picture Maggie being the more aggressive one even though she's much younger than you."

"Three years isn't so much," Luke remarked. His eyes were filled with humor and tenderness. "And my sister is a lot like Nora in her personality. She's a woman of action. If she thinks something should be done, she makes every effort to see that it is done. Soon.''

The truth in Luke's statement rang in her ears. Julianne's heart thudded loudly, sadly against her rib case. "Even with us," she conceded in little more than a whisper. "Our being together—that was Maggie's idea.''

Luke studied the sudden seriousness of Julianne's expression. How could anyone look so sad and so lovely, all at the same time? "In the beginning, it may have been Maggie who planted the thought in our minds, but it's becoming more all on its own.''

Julianne swallowed. Unable to find the words she needed, she nodded her head in mute agreement while Luke's eyes held her still. A sudden ripple of awareness washed over her, reminding her how quickly this was becoming more. The rest of her life was what she'd promised to this man who sat across the room from her, and he had done the same.

Luke looked away from Julianne but with obvious effort. His voice was low and unsteady when he spoke. "I'll go to church with you and the children in the morning, if you're planning to attend.''

"Yes, we're going," Julianne replied, "and I'd like it very much if you came along. So would Nora and Todd.'' She noticed the grandfather clock that stood in the corner of the living room. "Nine? Is that the correct time?''

Luke's mouth curved into an acknowledging smile. "Feels later, doesn't it?'' he commented.

"Spending the day at an amusement park with a couple of kids has a way of doing that to a person."

"Yes," Julianne agreed quietly. "But I'm glad we took them there. It made the day more special for them."

"The most special thing they'll remember about this day is that you married me. You belong here with us now. You're not a visitor anymore. Not that you ever really seemed like one."

"Honestly?" The one-word question came from her heart. "Because I didn't feel like one, Luke, except maybe that first day I watched the children for you. Other than that, I've had this odd sense of belonging here."

His voice echoed her sentiment. "Me, too. I was amazed how easily the children were drawn to you. Remember how they went to you that first morning? I left the center to go to work and neither one of them was crying—first time in over a year. It seemed like a miracle."

"Maybe it was," she said, her voice a little shakier than she would have liked. "Did you ever consider the possibility?"

Luke studied her with curious intensity. "No, I didn't. I guess I don't think in those terms anymore."

"Maybe you could, again, someday," she heard herself say, against her better judgment. Julianne meant to lower her gaze from his, but she couldn't just then. There was a flicker of something in his gaze. Recognition, possibly, that miracles do still happen?

But Luke looked away without responding, and an

uncomfortable silence fell over the room. Julianne caught her lower lip between her teeth until it throbbed. Luke had been away from the Lord for a very long time, she knew, but he still didn't seem to be ready for all of the trusting and believing it would take to come back. Just walking into a church tomorrow morning would probably be enough of a challenge for him.

She picked up her drink in one hand and her tennis shoes in the other. "I think I'll go upstairs," she said softly. "I'll check on the children before I go to bed."

"All right," Luke answered and stood up to walk with her to the staircase. "I know this seems...a little awkward, Julianne, but it won't always feel that way."

"I know. It will take time." She nodded her head, her blond hair swinging loosely against her neck. Julianne started to go up the steps when a strong hand gently squeezed her shoulder. As she turned to face Luke, her mouth curved into a soft and loving smile. "I forgot to say good-night, didn't I?"

But Luke didn't answer. Instead, he touched his mouth against the soft hair at her temple in a warm kiss. "I'm very aware of all that you're giving up to be my wife, to raise Nora and Todd." His eyes swept over her face with a tenderness in his expression that brought a mist of tears to Julianne's dark brown eyes. "Thank you for the promises we made today. I'll do everything I can to keep them."

"Me, too," she whispered. Then, raising up on her tiptoes, she kissed his cheek. "Good night, my husband.'' With a deep and unsteady breath, she moved away from him and hurried up the steps.

Entering the children's room, she found them sleeping peacefully. After kissing them both, she headed for the refuge of her own room. She closed the door and leaned back against it momentarily as she surveyed the contents of the bedroom. All her belongings were crowded into the space, except for a few larger items which Luke had stored in his garage. Even her goldfish swam silently in new surroundings on a long, narrow dresser. Julianne felt as if her whole life was represented by the things in this room. They had made her apartment into her home. Now, they were packed together here in this one small corner of the O'Hara house.

Just for a moment, Julianne's heart pounded in acknowledgment of what she'd done. She'd married a man she barely knew, agreed to a lifetime commitment of raising two young children, turned everything in her life upside down to become a mother, now, at age twenty-five. Her own parents had warned against this, Reverend Ben had been critical of the idea, but she'd done it, anyway. Now, here she was spending her wedding night alone, in a room filled with things from a life she'd left behind.

She sat down in the rocking chair in the corner to think. Being a major part of Nora and Todd's lives was exactly what Julianne wanted. She longed for it in a way Ben Hunter or her parents would never understand, and she'd achieved it. As for Luke...he could fall in love with her, just as she was already falling in love with him. Hadn't she felt that only moments ago? His gentle touch, a tender look. Her mind went back to the wedding ceremony, to Luke looking, really looking, into her eyes a moment longer than necessary before kissing her. What, she wondered, had he seen in her gaze that he didn't want to look away from? Hopefulness. Promises. Commitment. Julianne smiled. The same things she'd seen in his.

Chapter Ten

"**Y**our toast is ready. Come on, kids. Hurry up or you'll be late," Luke called out to his son and daughter, then picked up a cup of coffee from the kitchen table and took a drink. He looked toward the stove, where Julianne stood in a white bathrobe spreading butter on two slices of toasted bread. The robe, her old slippers and that early-morning ponytail did nothing to change the opinion he'd formed of his wife in the first days of their marriage. She was the most beautiful woman he'd ever met.

"Thank you, Julianne," Luke said and set his coffee down.

She looked up to see his smile. "For what?"

"For handling all of this. It's been almost a month, and we haven't scared you off yet." He hesitated, wondering if he should tell her the rest of this thoughts. He may as well be honest. "Those first couple of days, I had this sinking feeling that you'd leave for work one morning and never come back."

"I have to come back in the evening, Luke. I'm Nora and Todd's ride home," she answered with a soft laugh. "And, anyway, I was born for a life like this. I grew up in a household with six children, remember? Two at a time isn't much of a challenge."

"Maybe not to you, but for me—" Luke let his sentence die out. He looked toward the living room as the twins, still in their pajamas, came straggling in to have their breakfast. Todd had his usual smile on his cheerful face and his basset hound tucked under one arm.

"Hi, Daddy!" the boy exclaimed and went scrambling for a hug from his father while Nora climbed up onto a kitchen chair in silence.

"Morning, son," Luke picked Todd up and carried him over to where he could deposit him gently on a chair next to his sister. Then Luke playfully pulled on Nora's brown curls. "Morning, sunshine."

"Good morning," she said in a sleepy voice and yawned before picking up a piece of toast covered lightly with grape jelly. "Yummm. Grape's my favorite," she remarked.

"I know," Julianne answered and walked over to give each child a kiss on top of the head. "Scrambled eggs will be ready in a minute."

"I've gotta go," Luke said. He glanced toward the lunch box his wife had left on the counter for him. It was only one of the innumerable things she did for him. For them. A profound sense of gratitude engulfed Luke, nearly overwhelmed him right there in the kitchen. He blinked hard to fight a sudden surge of emotion. "Julianne," he began in an unsteady voice, "I...I'm so thankful to have you."

Julianne met her husband's gaze in surprise. She smiled. "I'm thankful, too, Luke. I love being a part of your life."

They stood there, looking at each other a moment too long before Luke said, "Well, I do need to go to work. I'll see you for dinner."

"Have a good day," Julianne offered and watched her husband disappear through the door. She smiled to herself. Something was happening between them. It was subtle, but it was real. She'd felt it in a dozen different little things—from the way he'd kissed her good-night that first night of their marriage to the way he usually reached for her hand to hold while they took evening walks with the kids.

She glanced out the window over her kitchen sink to see Luke getting into his truck. He looked as good in his jeans and a work shirt as he did in his dress clothes, which she had rarely seen. Luke had attended church with them only once since they'd officially become a family. After that first Sunday, he'd said nothing more about it, and Julianne was hesitant about asking...until now. The daily devotional she'd read earlier in the morning had stressed the importance of attending church as a family. She would ask Luke to go to services with them this week. He had promised he would attend church with them "occasionally," whatever that meant. Maybe, now, he would be ready to go again.

"Julianne, can I have coffee?" Nora asked while looking toward the cup her father had left behind.

"Sorry, sweetie. The coffee was for Dad only." Julianne reached for the cup and placed it in the sink. "Who is ready for scrambled eggs?"

"Me!" exclaimed Todd. But Nora sat silently with her pouty lip stuck out.

"Nora? Aren't you hungry?" The golden pile of eggs that Julianne slid onto Todd's plate must have looked pretty good to Nora because she immediately wanted some of her own.

"Me, too, please," she requested and the first bite brought a happier look to her sleepy eyes.

"Okay, kids, we forgot to pray. Todd, will you do that for us?" Julianne placed the skillet back on the stove and bowed her head for Todd's prayer. It was short and sweet.

Soon they had finished their breakfast, and Julianne guided the twins toward their bedroom to change out of their pajamas.

"Daddy always helps us a lot. I mean, a whole bunch," Nora remarked as she slid her arms into the sundress Julianne was pulling down over the girl's head. "With buttons and zippers and stuff."

"But much of this you could do yourself," Julianne responded. "Bring me your shoes, hon, and I'll show you."

So Nora picked up a pair of scuffed brown sandals that were stuck under her small bed. "Here," she said, handing them to Julianne.

"Okay now, put your finger here..." Julianne proceeded to show Nora how to slip her feet into the sandals without help. "We need to go shopping for some new shoes soon. These are nearly worn out,"

Julianne commented before turning to assist Todd with the sock he was struggling to slide onto his little foot.

"There you go." Then Julianne stood up. "Now, I need to get dressed. Go downstairs for a few minutes and wait for me. There's a Bible video in the VCR. All you need to do is press the play button."

She'd barely finished her sentence before the children ran for the stairs.

"Walk, please," Julianne called after them which brought Nora to a complete standstill. She turned to smile at her new stepmother with wide blue eyes that looked so much like her father's.

"That sounds nicer," she said.

"What does?" Julianne asked curiously.

"'Walk, please.' That's politer than 'Don't run!' like Daddy yells."

Julianne gave a soft laugh. "I guess it is. Maybe we can talk him into saying it, too. You think?"

"Nope," Nora responded. "Dad won't change."

Julianne watched Nora's slow descent of the steps with sadness slowly settling over her like a cloud. "Dad won't change." In how many ways was that true? Would he ever find his way back to the Lord he no longer trusted? Would his heart ever mend enough to someday belong to Julianne?

She walked into her bedroom and pulled a skirt and blouse from her closet. Her bedroom; her closet. Not theirs, she thought with a sigh. She looked at the narrow twin bed shoved into the corner of the room. A married woman. That's what she was now. Almost? Kind of? Shaking her head, she removed her bathrobe and hung it up on the hook inside the door. No, it was real. She was married and responsible for twin four-year-olds who made whatever awkward circumstances existed, worth it all. That was the part she needed to focus on, not the husband she'd gained in the arrangement—no matter how attracted she was to him.

Her daily interaction with Luke was confirming what she'd suspected all along. Luke O'Hara was as good and kind a man as Julianne had ever known. In fact, at times he reminded her a little of her own father. He took time with his children, listened to them, played with them frequently. She saw less and less of the workaholic brother Maggie had described to her before Luke and the twins moved to Fairweather. He had not worked a single Saturday since he finished the landscaping project for a chain of banks in Minneapolis. The last three jobs Luke accepted were in Baylor's Landing, and one of them was big. There was an undeveloped portion of acreage around Baylor Lake that the community had voted to turn into a picnic and camping area. Luke had been hired to make improvements on the grounds which covered many acres.

Sliding her forest-green skirt into place, she then buttoned her white short-sleeved blouse quickly. Moving in here with Luke and the children had been a surprisingly smooth transition. She and Luke had encountered very little uneasiness after that first night. Living here seemed as natural, although noisier, than it had at her own apartment.

She had promised Luke forever and the more she knew him, the more comfortable she felt with the promise she'd made. Living together worked well for all of them, especially the children who seemed much happier both at home and at the center, Julianne had noticed. They were changing, growing daily, and she was deeply grateful to God for allowing her to be a part of the process.

Her daily prayer was that she would be a positive influence on Nora and Todd all her life, in whatever she did. With God's help, she knew she had that capability. Without it, she would not. How Luke could think he could raise these children without the Lord's help, was beyond her understanding. She ran a brush through her hair, and within minutes, she and the children were headed toward their day at the center.

"Good morning, Julianne! Hi, Nora, Todd," the director of the center greeted the trio as they entered the building early that morning.

"Good morning, Mrs. Anderson," Nora offered as Todd said a quiet hi.

"Hello, Betty. How are you?" Julianne asked. She pulled open the door to her classroom so the children could go inside.

"I'm well, thank you," Betty replied. She adjusted her glasses while watching the kids run into the empty room. "So, how's life with the O'Haras?" The question was quietly asked once the twins were out of hearing range.

"It's great. The kids are happy, Betty. They're really doing well."

"And how about you? Is everything okay?"

"Yes," Julianne said. "I'm fine. Really." She placed her tote bag and straw purse on the floor by her desk. Looking up, she was surprised to see the look of concern that brought a slight frown to Betty's face. "Why?"

"I've been thinking about you a lot lately," Betty admitted. "Truth is, I think the Lord has put you on my mind deliberately, Julianne. I'm worried about you."

It was Julianne's turn to frown. "Why? Everything is going well for me right now. There's nothing to worry about."

Betty glanced toward the children and watched them dump large pieces of a puzzle onto a table in the far corner of the room. "I rarely get a chance to speak with you about anything other than the day care. It seems there aren't enough hours in the day anymore now that I'm helping my daughter plan her wedding. Rachel is so excited about the big day. But there's been something I wanted to talk to you about, Julianne. I've know you for several years, and I consider you my friend. That's why I feel comfortable saying this to you. I've been seeing Warren for a while, as you know, and I've already dealt with some of the issues you're dealing with now."

Folding her hands in front of her to keep from fidgeting, Julianne nodded her head. She suddenly knew what Betty was referring to. "Loving a man who has lost the wife he loved," she stated quietly.

Warren Sinclair had been a widower since sometime last year.

Betty nodded. "Has he called you by her name yet?"

"No." Julianne winced at the thought. "I hope it never happens."

"It could, you know. And you'll need to forgive him when he does because there's no way he'll be able to tell you how sorry he is." Betty paused. "How about photos of her? Have you come across many?"

"There used to be a framed picture of him and Kimberly together that was sitting on the dresser in the kids' room. But it disappeared sometime before the wedding. Now, there's a picture of just Kimberly. By herself."

"Good. That's easier to deal with."

"I want the children to remember their mother, Betty. She deserves that, and the twins need that," Julianne defended. "I wouldn't feel right without helping them keep their memories of her alive."

Betty nodded and placed a hand on Julianne's shoulder in a motherly touch. "It will all get easier as time goes by. Warren lost his first wife a little over a year ago. Believe me, I know how it feels to live in someone else's shadow. But it can be done. And happily. Just pray about it. And be patient."

"We've only been married such a short time, Betty. I don't expect miracles overnight," Julianne explained.

"Good. Some things take time, and this is one of them." She gave Julianne's arm a squeeze. "Warren would be glad to talk to Luke sometime. If you think he'd be interested.''

"From what I've heard from Emma, Warren's faith was actually strengthened by his loss. I wish Luke's reaction could have been the same.''

"Everyone's different, I realize, but Luke could probably benefit from Warren's wisdom. Let me know if you want to try to get them together.''

Julianne nodded. "I'll keep it in mind." She glanced back at the kids but they were engrossed in their own conversation and paying no attention to the two women. "Is my assistant today going to be Laura or Lisa?''

"Lisa. She'll be here by eight." Betty turned to exit the room. "If you want to talk, Julianne, let me know. Any time.''

"Thanks," she replied and watched her friend walk toward the doorway. "Betty? You referred to Warren's 'first' wife." She smiled and raised an eyebrow in question. "Does that mean there is soon to be a second?''

"Possibly," Betty responded, her face brightening as she spoke. "Time will tell.''

Time. Julianne glanced down at her watch to see it fast approaching seven. She picked up a stack of construction paper of assorted colors and began distributing them around the arts and crafts table. She had another busy day ahead of her, and it was about to begin whether she was ready, or not.

The chicken-noodle casserole Julianne had prepared was in the oven, staying warm while she watched anxiously out the kitchen window for Luke's truck to enter the driveway. "It's seventhirty. Luke, where are you?" she whispered to herself. The children were playing house in the living room. Nora was cooking up a pretend pot of soup and Todd was setting their little plastic table with the set of toy dinnerware Julianne had picked up for them at the variety store yesterday. Both children were totally engrossed in their play, and Julianne was relieved. That way, they wouldn't see how upset she was at the moment. Luke had never been this late coming home, and there had been no call to warn her of a change in plans, so she had no recourse but to worry. So she did.

Releasing the curtain, she walked over to the dishwasher and began to load it with the dirty dishes from the supper she'd eaten with the children. Maybe if she kept busy, she'd worry less about her tardy husband. Where was he and why hadn't he called? She'd finished that job and was deciding what to do next when, finally, she heard the sound of the truck pulling up outside. Exhaling a sigh of relief, she pulled a tray of ice out of the freezer to fill Luke's glass. He'd probably be hungry, unless he'd already eaten someplace else.

"Hi," Luke offered quietly when he entered the back door. "Sorry I'm so late."

"Daddy's home!" Both kids came running before Julianne could reply. She picked up Luke's dinner plate and put some of the casserole on it along with green beans and a dinner roll. Then she filled his glass.

Within minutes, the kids were back at their play in the adjoining room, and Julianne was putting leftovers into the refrigerator.

"I really am sorry, Julianne," Luke reiterated. "We were just ready to leave for the day when the owner of the complex showed up and wanted to see how things were going. Then he wanted to show us another job that he'd like us to work on when we're finished with the first one. The place was clear across town. I had no idea it was going to take so long, and I'd forgotten to take my phone to work with me this morning."

Julianne was standing by the sink, rinsing dishes and trying desperately to suppress the anger swelling up within her. She was so upset she could barely speak.

"You could have called," she said quietly, angrily.

"I should have. I thought I'd call you when I got back to the truck. Then I realized I'd left my phone here at the house this morning. I had no idea we'd be gone so long," Luke attempted an honest explanation that, from the expression on her face, he knew wasn't going over well. "You and the kids ate already, didn't you? I wouldn't want you waiting on me—"

"Of course, we ate," she snapped, startling both of them with her uncharacteristically sharp words. "You can't keep four-year-olds waiting this long."

Luke stood there, not sure how to repair whatever damage he'd done. If she was furious with him, she had reason to be. He hadn't considered how upset this might make her.

"Eat your supper while I give the kids their bath and get them to bed." This time she spoke in a more restrained voice. She left him in the kitchen to eat alone. She was too angry, too frightened by what had happened to stay there with him another minute. Soon she had both kids in the tub with bubbles and plastic bath toys everywhere. By the time their bath was over, Luke was finished with his meal and he was upstairs to kiss the children good-night. Once that was done, Julianne hurried downstairs toward the kitchen and away from Luke. And he wasn't far behind her.

"Julianne, wait," he said. "Please." Luke reached forward and caught her arm gently in his hand. "Don't be angry."

"You scared me!" she lashed out at him as she turned to face him. "You should have called. I thought you'd been in an accident or something, Luke. You frightened me." Tears filled her eyes. She didn't know whether to hug him in celebration that he was all right or throw something at him for alarming her so badly.

"I know, I know," he agreed. "I'm sorry. It was stupid of me not to call but I just had no idea I'd be this late. Or that you'd be this upset." The apologetic expression on his face did little to soothe her frayed nerves, so he pulled gently on the arm he had within his grasp, taking her easily into his arms. "Julianne, I'm sorry. I didn't mean to frighten you. Forgive me," he spoke gentle words as he held her close while she wept.

"I kept thinking...what if you don't come home? What are we going to do without you? The kids aren't ready to be left with just me. They'll never be ready for that."

Luke smiled. She could feel the sudden curve of his mouth against her temple. "The children love you, Julianne. If anything happens, they'll be fine with you."

"But you can't trust me with that responsibility. They're your children."

"They're yours, too, now," Luke assured her and rubbed his cheek against the soft blond hair that framed her face. "I'd trust you with them more than anyone."

Julianne tilted her head, wordlessly, to look up into his serious expression.

"That's why I married you, Julianne. You're the one they love, the one we need. I think I knew that right from the start." He studied the wistful look in her eyes. "Don't you know that by now?"

She shook her head no at first, then shrugged. "I don't know, Luke. All I really know is that I'm thankful you're okay. I was so afraid I'd lost you. I was so scared."

Luke didn't respond. He couldn't just then, because all he could think of was how much he wanted to kiss this lovely woman in his arms. His wife.

"Julianne," he spoke her name tenderly as his hands eased into the softness of her hair, cupping her face and drawing her to him. His warm mouth met hers in a firm, slow exchange, and she kissed him with all the sweet longing in her heart.

When Julianne recaptured her breath, words rushed from her in a mere whisper against his lips. "Luke, I don't want to lose you. Please. Not ever."

"You haven't lost me. I'm here, I'm all right," he answered quietly. He longed to assure her that he'd always be there for her. Always. Forever. That's what his heart wanted, but it wasn't a promise that was his to give, he knew too well. His blood ran cold. It was a promise he and Kimberly had childishly made to each other years ago; one she couldn't keep. He stood perfectly still, remembering.

"Luke?" Julianne spoke his name softly, then noticed his guarded expression. She started to pull slightly away from him. "Is something wrong?"

Hot tears stung his eyes. He cleared his throat harshly and let his wife slowly slip from his grasp. "No, I'm okay. I'm sorry, tonight isn't the right time for this, Julianne. You were angry, upset...afraid I'd been hurt or worse. That's what started this."

Julianne listened in silence, watching the moment pass in Luke's eyes. He'd gone from wanting her— she was sure of it—to releasing her, and she'd seen it all in the endless depths of his eyes. What she couldn't see was—why? What had she done wrong? And would their time come someday? To stay?

Chapter Eleven

"Luke," Julianne called his name as she knocked on his bedroom door. "Please wake up. Frank's on the phone." She knocked again and then opened the door an inch or two. "Luke, please wake up."

"What's wrong?" he asked when he finally awakened from a deep sleep to hear his name being called.

"It's something about Maggie. Frank is calling from the hospital, and he wants to speak with you. He's very upset."

Luke grabbed a robe and was up and out of the room in seconds. Picking up the extension in the living room, he then glanced at the clock. It was 1:00 a.m. "Frank? What is it? Is Maggie all right?"

The broken voice of his brother-in-law on the other end of the phone awakened Luke completely. Something had to be wrong—terribly wrong—for Frank to be nearly unable to speak.

"Frank, listen to me. Calm down and tell me what's going on."

"It's the baby. Maggie is in premature labor, and I don't think they can stop it. It's too soon, Luke. Much too soon for—" The sentence ended abruptly.

"Frank? What's going on? Can you still hear me?" Luke persisted, wishing he were already in the Minneapolis hospital so he could see his sister for himself to find out how serious this was.

"Luke, her doctor is walking this way. I've got to go. Come as soon as you can, and bring Julianne. Maggie needs her."

"We'll be there," Luke replied. He hung up the receiver as his mind raced with details. They'd have to find someone to take the twins so he and Julianne could both go to the hospital. "Juli—" he started to call her name and then turned to see her standing at the bottom of the staircase, waiting.

"How bad is it?" she asked quietly.

"Maggie is in premature labor. It looks like they may not be able to stop it."

Julianne's gasp was muffled by the hand she raised to cover her mouth. "Oh, no, Luke. After all her excitement, all the planning. This can't happen to Maggie."

"Well, it's happening, and we need to get dressed and get over to the hospital as soon as we can." Luke switched on a nearby lamp. "I'll get the kids up. Do you think Betty Anderson would watch them if we took them to her house?"

"Maybe, but let me call Reverend Ben first. He's closer. He might be willing to come over here so the kids can go on sleeping. There's no reason to wake them if we don't have to."

"Reverend Ben—a baby-sitter?" Luke asked in surprise.

"He's great with the twins, Luke. He does Children's Church with them every Sunday, he sees them at the center every day and they're very fond of him."

"Okay," Luke agreed but with some hesitation. "I'll trust your judgment on this. Do you want to call him, or should I?"

"I'll do it. Why don't you get dressed and find the truck keys."

He frowned momentarily. "Keys?"

"I see you searching for them practically every morning. Try the kitchen counter by the coffeemaker. I think that's where I last saw them." Then she grabbed up the phone and dialed.

His frown remained as he watched her place the call to Ben Hunter. Then he started up the stairs toward the bedrooms.

Soon Julianne was passing his bedroom again, hurrying down the hallway toward her own room to change. She knocked on his door lightly. Then she whispered as loudly as she could without risk of waking the twins. "Ben will be here in about twenty minutes. I told him he could go ahead and sleep on the couch for several hours since the kids probably won't be awake until about seven. I'll be ready by the time Ben gets here."

When Luke pulled open the door, he was fully dressed in tan slacks and a knit golf shirt, and he seemed more awake now than he had a few minutes earlier. "I forgot to shave."

"It doesn't matter," Julianne responded, reaching up to touch his cheek. "You look fine. Honestly." Then she pulled her hand away. "You always look good with a five o'clock shadow."

"This is more like one o'clock shadow," he said with a shake of his head. "And I still have to find those keys."

"Kitchen counter. Coffeemaker. Remember?"

"Yes. I'll probably have time to make coffee before Ben gets here."

"Good idea," she said and hurried toward her own bedroom. "I'll be downstairs in a few minutes."

She pulled open her closet and pulled out her denim jumper and a T-shirt. Dressing quickly, she slid into a pair of sandals and headed for the bathroom to do something with her hair. The something she decided on was a ponytail. Then came five minutes of makeup before she brushed her teeth, checked on the sleeping children and then headed downstairs toward the smell of fresh brewing coffee.

"No Ben yet?" she asked when she entered the kitchen.

"Not yet," Luke replied. He reached to switch on the outside lights. "There's a cup of tea on the table for you."

"Thank you," she said, pleasantly surprised. "I thought I'd have to settle for coffee."

"I don't want you to have to 'settle' for anything," Luke remarked quietly before reaching for his own cup.

Julianne added some honey to her hot drink and stirred it with the spoon Luke had laid out for her.

He didn't sound like his usual self. Of course, it was the middle of the night and he was worried about his sister, Julianne realized. Maybe that was all there was to it. Maybe she should change the subject. "I'll drive to Minneapolis if you're tired. I don't mind."

"No, I'll do it," he said. Just then a knock came on the kitchen door, and Luke opened the door to allow a rather disheveled-looking Reverend Hunter inside the house.

"Thanks for coming," Julianne said.

"Any more news on Maggie?" he asked, looking toward Luke for an answer.

"Not yet. We'll let you know as soon as we find out something. And we really do appreciate your coming over here like this, Reverend Hunter. Letting the children stay in their own beds makes it much easier on us." Then Luke glanced toward his wife. "Ready?"

"Yes, just let me show Ben the kids' room and the bathroom."

"That's okay. I'll find my own way around, Julianne. Go see Maggie."

"Thanks, Ben," she said with a smile. "I put a bed pillow and a sheet on the couch for you. Nora and Todd won't be awake until around seven." Then she looked toward her husband. "Ready?"

He gave an affirmative answer with a tip of his head and they headed out the kitchen door.

The first few miles of the drive to the hospital, they didn't talk much. Julianne was silently praying for Maggie, the friend who had become her sister-in-law. "Just think," she said softly, "I'll actually be an aunt to my best friend's baby. Thanks to marrying you," she added with a gentle smile and looked toward Luke. But he wasn't smiling.

"She'll be okay, Luke. Even if the worst happens."

"And it could," he commented quietly, deliberately.

"It could, but if she loses the baby, certainly Maggie would get through it somehow. Try not to worry too much until we get there."

Julianne stared out the window as they drove the twenty miles into the city in the early hours of the morning. Her prayers were centered on Maggie and the baby, but once or twice she found herself praying for her own situation. For the child she'd never carry inside her. She wanted a baby—Luke's baby—now more than ever. The stark reality of that longing hadn't fully hit her until this moment. How, she wondered, could she be so self-centered to dwell on her own desires when her friend needed her help now? Irritated with herself, she put her mind back on Maggie and began praying for her again. In fact, Julianne became so absorbed in reminding the Lord of Maggie's great need throughout the drive that she barely noticed Luke's solemn silence on the trip.

Another drive to a hospital. How he hated the journey. It always reminded him of Kimberly, of the many trips back and forth from their apartment to her hospital bedside during her illness. Losing her would always be a part of him, but it had seemed over the past few months that it was occupying a smaller space in his life than it had for the past year.

He was grateful for the freedom. Sometimes he felt like he could breathe deeply again. He could look out the window on a bright summer morning and actually think about what a beautiful day it was. That was something he'd never take for granted again. More and more his thinking was geared for the present. His kids, his work. His wife. He had to admit Julianne was responsible for much of his altered view of life. Her presence in their lives was a blessing. Daily. Everything from the frequent smiles she put on Nora and Todd's faces to the way she'd redecorated the kitchen so that it now looked like it belonged to a family. A real family. And whom did he have to thank for the blessing that Julianne was to them? Not himself; he was certain of that. He knew he'd been a bitter, grieving man when they'd met, and he'd brushed off her first hint of interest in him. No, if Julianne ever really loved him—not just his children, but him—it would be a miracle. Plain and simple. And miracles came from God. Whether Luke O'Hara liked admitting it or not.

"There's the hospital." Julianne's soft voice cut into his thoughts.

Luke glanced in her direction. Her blond hair was pulled back carelessly into a ponytail, her clothing was slightly wrinkled and she didn't have on a drop of that lovely perfume she usually wore...but she was the most beautiful sight he'd ever seen. Sitting right there, only a few feet away. Luke's heart ached within him. Why hadn't he seen it before now? He loved her. She was gentle and compassionate, tender and caring, and she'd sacrificed all that her life might have been for his children. For him. And he loved her. He'd never felt the emotion as acutely as he did then.

"Let's hurry," Julianne remarked. "There's the parking lot."

Luke returned his focus to the situation. He needed a parking space and to get into the hospital as quickly as they could. He loved Julianne and it must have been some kind of a miracle because he didn't think he would ever love anyone again. God had proved him wrong. In this instance, and in how many others?

Within moments, they were out of the truck and hurrying across the parking lot in the early morning darkness.

"I hope and pray she's okay," Julianne said more to herself than to Luke as they neared the front entrance.

"And I can only hope," Luke remarked in a low voice so filled with regret that it startled Julianne. She turned her head to look at him, studying his profile while they walked.

"You can pray, too," she said quietly keeping pace with his long strides. "All you need to do is try."

Without responding, Luke reached for the door to open it for Julianne but carefully avoided meeting her gaze.

Then it occurred to her how silent Luke had been on the drive to the hospital. She'd barely spoken to him for most of the trip. Her mind had been mostly on Maggie, and Luke had apparently been lost in his own thoughts. But, now she wondered, what kind of thoughts? Ones with eternal significance?

Luke cleared his throat harshly and pushed the button for the elevator, which opened immediately, offering them transportation to the fourth floor. To Maggie.

"Luke, are you all right?" Julianne asked regardless of the two orderlies that were sharing the elevator ride.

"Yes," he answered in an unsteady voice. "I'm fine," he lied. He hadn't felt this miserable in a long time. His sister needed him. Maggie and her unborn baby needed his help in a way he couldn't give. Prayer. Luke couldn't recall uttering a single prayer in over a year. Not since Kimberly's death. And he hadn't planned on starting again tonight.

When they arrived on the correct floor, the doors opened and they moved quickly toward the nurses' desk.

"We're here to see Maggie Wren."

"Mrs. Wren is in 427 at the end of the hallway, but her doctor is in with her now. If you could wait about ten minutes, that would be best. May I suggest waiting in the chapel at the end of the hallway? It's much more comfortable than our lobby."

Julianne glanced down the hallway as Luke did the same, and they both stood, speechless, looking at the chapel. Then, without comment, Luke headed in that direction with a determined stride, opened the doors and disappeared into the small hospital chapel. Julianne's hand flew to her mouth in surprise. Maybe Maggie's struggle tonight would result in Luke facing his need for Christ in his life again. Maybe Julianne would see answers to her prayers for her husband, tonight, in this hospital. She glanced toward the dozen or so chairs in the lobby. Her first impulse was to have a seat there and wait, giving Luke the privacy he needed. But while making her way over to the sitting area, the notion of leaving him alone disappeared, replaced with a strong impression that she should join him. Following instinct instead of logic, she approached the double doors she'd seen her husband disappear through earlier. Taking a deep breath and whispering a prayer, she opened a door and stepped inside.

The lighting in the room was subtle, adding to the sense of privacy of this place. The ivory walls and polished oak floor reminded Julianne of her home church...until she looked toward the front of the chapel and saw something she'd never seen at The Old First Church: Luke at a narrow wooden altar. Kneeling. Tears began to trickle from her eyes and she wiped at them with her fingers as she walked down the center aisle toward the altar where she carefully, quietly knelt next to her silent husband.

Her heart raced with concern. Should she say something? Should she offer some scripture verses that would guide him, help him to find his way back to the spiritual life he'd lost? "Be still and know that I am God." That was the verse from Psalms that came to her mind and refused to leave. Be still. Be still.

She placed her hands on the altar railing and knelt by Luke's side without breathing a word. She had no more than settled into her place by his side, when Luke reached over, covering both of her hands with one of his own, without looking up. Then she moved closer, leaning her head against his shoulder in a tender moment, just as the flood of tears Luke had held back for too long, let go. His face was buried against one arm as he leaned against the altar railing and wept, his breathing strained, his heart broken, and Julianne knelt there with him, her head pressed against his shoulder, praying silently through her tears.

Much of his prayer was indistinguishable to Julianne, but she did hear Kimberly's name spoken a time or two which only increased her own flow of tears. He'd loved Kimberly. She'd always known that, and she clearly recalled she'd cried buckets over Craig Johnson when he'd left her. But some of that crying had helped clear a fresh pathway to her heart—the pathway Luke had taken. She knew that was what Luke needed, too. To cry his heart out over Kimberly. Only then would there be room in that heart for her.

When the tears subsided and Luke quieted, Julianne reached behind the altar for a box of tissues she'd caught a glimpse of and handed him several. Luke accepted them and wiped his eyes. He'd received the forgiveness, the acceptance he'd needed from God, and he felt about a decade younger than he had when he first knelt there.

"Everything okay?" she asked in a voice barely above a whisper when his reddened eyes met her watery gaze.

He smiled, nodding his head, and reached for Julianne, hugging her close to him. "Yes, finally, everything's going to be fine," he replied, his voice hoarse. "Thank you for coming. I needed you here. With me," he added, speaking warm words against her ear. He held her so tightly, she could barely breathe, but she didn't mind. She just offered a silent word of thanks to the Lord for prompting her to join her husband in the chapel.

"Now," Luke said, releasing her. "We've got to find out about Maggie and the baby."

Just then the doors at the back of the chapel opened and Frank Wren stuck his head inside. "I wondered where you two were." Then he noticed Luke's eyes and, maybe, the changed expression on his brother-in-law's face. From silent grief to a look of hope. "Luke," Frank began and then glanced at Julianne, who was smiling broadly. "What's going on?"

"I just came in here to pray for my sister," Luke answered matter-of-factly.

"Pray?" Frank asked, bewildered but pleased. "That's wonderful. That's great. Maggie will be so happy to hear your news."

"How is Maggie?" Luke interrupted. "And the baby?"

"*Much* better," Frank said with a dramatic sigh of relief. "She's going to leave her job and take it easy for the rest of her pregnancy, but the labor pains have stopped and she's resting comfortably right now. Come and see her."

Maggie's complexion was pale and dark circles

shadowed her lively blue eyes when the three of them entered her private room at the other end of the hallway.

"How are you, honey?" Frank asked immediately and began adjusting the blanket that covered her. "Do you want something to drink?"

"No, I'm fine, Frank. Really. And, Luke, it's so sweet of you and Julianne to come here in the middle of the night." Maggie spoke quietly as though she were exhausted. "I shouldn't have been such a wimp, asking Frank to call you out of bed at an hour like this. Where are the twins?"

"Reverend Ben is with them. We didn't even wake them up since he could come over. He's probably asleep on the sofa right now," Julianne explained. She slipped her arm through Luke's and held on tightly as her heart swelled with love for her husband. He even looked different. Younger, happier, lighter in spirit. And it only made her love him more.

Luke was smiling, a wide, generous smile that Maggie took note of while Julianne was talking. "What's up with you, big brother? You're smiling as though you have a secret. It reminds me of when we were kids and you'd try to keep something from me."

"No real secrets," he assured her. "I'm just thankful to God that you and your baby are going to be okay."

Maggie stared at him wordlessly.

"I feel free, Maggie and about ten years younger," Luke said. "I finally had to admit to the

Lord once again that I really do have an eternal soul, and that I want it to belong to Him.''

Maggie's parched lips curved into a joyful smile, and Frank reached for her cup of ice to hand it to her. ''So Julianne finally got through to you?''

''It wasn't me,'' Julianne responded. ''It was all between Luke and the Lord. I was just there to pray for him when he needed it.''

''And I definitely needed it,'' Luke commented, then he quieted and his countenance changed slightly. From lighthearted to serious. ''I had to admit that I need to keep my life committed to God, even when I don't understand everything.'' He paused. ''That's not been easy.''

''I know,'' Maggie said softly. ''I know, Luke.'' She raised a hand, reaching toward her brother and he leaned forward, giving her a warm hug. ''I love you.''

''I love you, too, Maggie,'' he replied. ''Thanks for your prayers, and I'm so thankful both you and your baby are all right.''

''Me, too,'' Maggie answered before releasing him and seeing him return to Julianne's side, to take her hand in his. ''Now, if you'll forgive me…I've called you all here at this horrible hour of the morning just so I could tell you I'm exhausted and need my sleep. Could you please leave now?'' She smiled weakly, only half joking.

''Say no more,'' Julianne responded and without letting go of Luke's hand, she leaned forward to kiss her friend. ''Get some rest. We'll see you soon.''

''Not you, Frank,'' Maggie added her single exception to her request. "I need you here for moral support."

"I know, hon. I'm not going anywhere," Frank assured her.

"Let's go home," Luke said with a sigh and a smile, and they boarded the elevator to head back down to ground level where they soon located the truck. Home sounded awfully good. To both of them.

"Don't forget we have a wedding to attend this afternoon," Julianne commented while watching Luke climb into the driver's seat.

"That's right. Morgan Talbot and Rachel Anderson White. I'd forgotten all about it." He turned the key in the ignition and began to work his way out of the parking lot.

Julianne asked with a soft laugh. "Do you think we'll be able to stay awake during the ceremony?"

"Maybe, if we drink enough coffee," he answered. "And you'll have to convert to coffee. I don't think the caffeine in herbal tea will do the job."

They talked much more on this trip than they did on the drive to the hospital. Discussing things about their faith in the Lord came easily to both of them, and Julianne was grateful she had her husband, a man of like belief, to share that part of her life. Glancing in Luke's direction, she had the urge to slide over on the seat and sit next to him. She wanted more of him—his touch, his tenderness, his love. "Lord," she wondered silently to herself, "he's given his heart to You, but isn't there a place, somewhere, in that heart for me, too?" The ride home suddenly seemed long until they neared Fairweather.

"I'm sorry for the times I've let you down, Julianne," Luke said quietly. "I've argued with you about God, about your faith. I apologize for letting my own anger, my own disbelief try to influence your thinking."

"We very rarely argue about anything, Luke. And I certainly forgive you for whatever it is you think you've done wrong," she answered and stared out the window into the darkness of early morning hours. "Your heart is right with God, that's all that matters now." Then she paused. "You will go to church with us, won't you?"

"Yes," he promised, keeping his eyes on the traffic. "I will, and I'll help you with your Sunday school class if you would like me to."

"Are you serious?" She turned her head to see his smiling profile. Then she tucked some loose strands of hair back into her ponytail clasp. "Third and fourth graders? You'd be interested in doing that?"

"Sure. Those are the grades I used to teach back at the church I attended in Chicago."

Chicago. Julianne's heart felt its familiar sting of jealousy. Luke had experienced a whole life she knew little of. But then, she reminded herself quickly, she had done the same, hadn't she? College, teaching, her engagement and near marriage to Craig Johnson? Yet, she only rarely had the sense that Luke was jealous of anything in her past.

"May I ask you something?" Luke spoke hesitantly, giving the distinct impression that he wasn't sure he should pursue this matter.

"Sure. Go ahead." She waited.

"How did you know Reverend Hunter's phone number this morning? Without looking it up?"

"It's easy to remember," she answered. "It's just one digit away from the day care's main number. Why?"

"I just wondered," he responded.

Then she understood. He'd wondered if she'd called Ben frequently enough, in the past or in the present, to have the number memorized. Julianne smiled and returned her gaze to the scenery outside her window. He was jealous. At least, a little. That was a good sign from a husband.

Now, if Julianne could just get through Rachel and Morgan Talbot's wedding without sobbing, she'd be eternally grateful. Watching the bride join her groom at the altar wouldn't be easy. The newlywed Talbots' love for each other would be obvious, open, radiant. Julianne sighed softly. Would it ever be that way for the O'Haras?

Chapter Twelve

The wedding of Rachel Anderson White and Morgan Talbot, M.D., was one of the biggest events of the summer in Fairweather, Minnesota. The impressive white clapboard structure of the church with its classic double-door entrance and tall steeple proved a splendid setting for a nearly perfect wedding. The traditional decor of the sanctuary with its stained-glass windows and cream-colored walls looked elegant with Rachel's choice of summer flowers: daisies and roses. The yellow-and-white decorations reminded Julianne of her own bridal bouquet, and the thought did nothing to calm her uneasiness while she and Luke took their seats on the bride's side of the church.

Lovely music floated through the air. Luke made some passing comment about it although Julianne didn't pay attention to what he was saying. Instead, she concentrated on gratitude. In particular, her need to be grateful for the blessings she had. Two loving children playing happily now with their baby-sitter. A husband who had returned to his Christian beliefs after being too long astray. Good health. A great job. Caring friends. It was all in an attempt not to be jealous of what Rachel Anderson White was getting. A man who adored her and stood waiting at an altar full of flowers to pledge his eternal love.

Morgan Talbot looked handsome and calm, Julianne noticed, but Luke would have looked better in that tux with the teal cummerbund. The groom was looking toward the doorway through which Rachel would enter momentarily. Lindsay, Rachel's little girl from her previous marriage, had already appeared in a lacy yellow dress, tossing rose petals from a small wicker basket onto the pathway her mother would soon walk. Then the moment Julianne dreaded arrived. The traditional bridal music began and Julianne's heart pounded loudly in her ears. She and Luke stood together, as did the rest of the congregation, at the first glimpse of the beautiful bride.

Rachel Anderson White was an attractive young woman, Luke considered while all eyes rested on her as she made the long walk to the altar. But she wasn't half as beautiful as his own bride. He glanced over at Julianne, startled to see her pale complexion. He leaned close. "Julianne, are you all right?"

She nodded and forced a smile. *No,* she wanted to shout. *I'm not all right. I'll never truly be all right until you love me. Really love me the way Morgan loves Rachel.*

With Rachel's grand entrance complete, she joined

her groom at the front of the church and the congregation took their seats to watch the ceremony proceed. Julianne nervously twisted the tissue she held in her fingers while Reverend Ben spoke solemn words.

Ben had agreed to perform this wedding, as though Rachel's marriage were blessed by the Lord and her own was of questionable origin. Julianne's thoughts only added to her misery. Why should she agonize over this? Rachel had something she didn't have. Big deal. It wasn't like that was the first time in her life she'd experienced jealousy and it surely wouldn't be the last. Although, Julianne couldn't remember wanting anything she didn't have as much as she wanted the love of her husband. She blinked back hot tears. Concentrating on the promises Rachel and Morgan were audibly making to each other, Julianne attempted to maintain what fragile control she still had over her emotions.

Luke's strong hand squeezed hers in a reassuring caress. He gave her a sideways glance of concern, but it didn't ease her fear of bursting into tears, right there, in the middle of a formal wedding. She wanted to leave, but that, Julianne knew, wouldn't be good. Then rumors would fly in Fairweather. From Emma Fulton on. Everyone would speculate about what was wrong with Luke O'Hara's wife. Wasn't she happy with her new family?

Maybe Reverend Hunter had been right, they might say, to disapprove of the marriage? And how could Julianne ever explain that she was deliriously happy with her new life? With the kids, her home, the fine man that her husband was? That all she really wanted was more? Luke had given her everything except his heart—and that's what was breaking hers into tiny pieces. Now, in the middle of this lovely wedding.

Then the ceremony came to a close with a kiss between the bride and groom and a walk down the center aisle. Julianne breathed in slowly, deeply. Feeling a little calmer she slipped her arm through Luke's and they left the church to join other invited guests under the huge white canopies on the village green.

"Julianne," Luke asked quietly on their way to the tables spread with beautiful linen tablecloths and silver platters of food. "What's wrong? Would you rather not be here?"

"I'm fine, really," she lied and reached for a cup of lemonade from a nearby serving tray. After a sip or two, she'd convinced herself she could smile and make small talk for a while. Being polite had some importance to it, no matter how miserable she felt, and Betty would be disappointed if Julianne rushed out now, without celebrating the occasion with good friends.

The three-tiered cake was white with tiny yellow roses. It looked "heavenly" little Lindsay, who was hearing impaired, had declared in sign language and Julianne agreed. *Absolute perfection* was another phrase that would have been appropriate. Much like everything else about this event was turning out to be.

The receiving line moved slowly on that hot August afternoon, and the O'Haras greeted and congratulated Morgan and Rachel Talbot, wishing them much happiness. They exchanged only a few words before moving on to talk briefly to the mother of the bride, Betty Anderson, about the Lake Baylor fishing contest held last week in which she had bagged the big one—a twenty-three-inch bass all the fishermen had been envious of. By the time they'd finished talking and Luke had refilled Julianne's cup with lemonade, she'd forgotten most of what the conversation had been about. But her nerves were a little less jittery, and her sadness had eased a bit when the final bombshell hit. Warren Sinclair and Betty Anderson made a surprise announcement, at the encouragement of the bride, that they, too, would soon be getting married. Little Lindsay was smiling and dancing around the couple, but all Julianne could focus on was the look exchanged between Betty and Warren. Love. Pure and simple. Julianne felt ill.

"I'm sorry, Luke, but I have to go home," Julianne said in a voice barely above a whisper. "Can you pick up the kids?"

Luke accepted the half-empty cup Julianne handed back to him while studying her saddened expression. It was one he had seen before. "Aren't you feeling well?"

"No, I mean, yes, that's it," she latched on to the feeble excuse. "I don't feel well. I'll see you at home later." As she turned from him to hurry away from the festivities, she consoled herself with the thought that she wasn't really lying to him. She really did feel sick—sick of the way things were going...or *weren't* going would be more accurate.

Luke watched her rush away from him through the crowd toward the edge of the village green and begin the short walk toward their home. He placed their drinks on a nearby table and went after her. In only a moment or two, he was beside her, reaching for her arm to slow her pace.

"If you're sick, let me take you home. I can pick up the children later," he insisted.

"No, I'm fine. I mean, I'm not fine, but I can walk," she responded and pulled her arm gently away from him. She wanted desperately to be alone so she could cry, sulk, scream—whatever it was she needed to do to get this miserable jealousy out of her system. How could she have ever thought her situation might find its way to a storybook ending? A happily-ever-after ending? She must have been blind or stupid or...falling in love.

"Then I'll walk with you—" he offered.

"No, Luke, please." She stopped in her tracks and turned to face him. Her throat ached with despair, and she swallowed hard. "I really need to be alone, if you don't mind. Just for a little while." She tried to smile, but the effort was more than she could manage. "Please?"

Reluctance was evident in his questioning eyes and the continued frown on his face. What had he done to upset her? He didn't have a clue, and it had to be his fault. The children weren't even with them this afternoon. "Julianne, if I've said something wrong—"

"No, no, it's nothing like that," she assured him and raised a hand to his chest, straightening his tie with a gentle touch. "It's not you. It's me," she answered. "I need to think, maybe pray. I haven't done enough of that lately."

"If you haven't found enough free time for yourself because of the children, we can change that, Julianne. We'll work it out," he assured her and raised a hand to touch her cheek. "Won't you tell me what's bothering you?"

Julianne shook her head in dismay. How could she tell him the awful truth that happy weddings and beautiful brides made her sad? And that she was jealous of every woman who had ever borne a child? It sounded horrible—even to her! How much worse it would sound spoken aloud to Luke.

"Go back and enjoy the reception. Practically everyone in town is there. Congratulate Warren and Betty for me." She tried to keep her voice steady, but it was faltering.

"Not without you," he replied.

"But I really need a few minutes alone, Luke." She forced a halfhearted smile. "I'll be fine. We can talk later."

It took all her effort to turn and walk away from her husband, leaving him standing there on the south side of the village green wondering if his marriage was coming apart at the seams when he hadn't even been aware, until this moment, that Julianne was unhappy. She hadn't seemed sad lately. Not like she had been when he first met her. But maybe she had been, and he just hadn't wanted to acknowledge it or deal with it. Some things are easier to ignore than to accept.

Luke let her go as she requested. He didn't know what else to do. He stood watching her walk away, her long cotton dress of pastel colors growing smaller and smaller in the distance as his heart ached within him. Losing Julianne would be more than he could bear. He loved her. Deeply. He'd come face-to-face with that reality last night on the way to the hospital. His need for her was far greater than she knew, much more than he'd ever told her. Suddenly, he stopped breathing as stark realization hit him. The things she didn't know. That was the problem. He'd had every intention of telling her tonight when they were alone. After the kids were in bed. He'd bought a gift that morning he planned to give her when he explained his feelings. But later might be too late. She needed to know now.

Julianne did not slow her pace or glance back over her shoulder on her walk to the O'Hara house. She was afraid she'd find Luke coming after her, and she didn't want that. He would make it too easy to fall right into his arms and cry all over him again. Once was enough for that type of behavior. This time she was going to be more in control. Either that or fall apart completely and give the whole situation to God. There was the solution she needed, she knew. She hadn't turned this relationship over to the Lord. Holding back felt better because she feared she'd have to face the truth that Reverend Ben had tried to impress upon. Maybe marrying Luke was something she shouldn't have done. She didn't know anymore. How could she go to the Lord now and ask for His help? After she'd blundered right ahead with her life and done what she wanted?

"What have I done?" she moaned softly to herself as she entered the home and headed straight for her bedroom. "And, more importantly, what am I going to do about it?" she wondered aloud.

Taking off the summery dress she'd worn to Rachel's wedding, she slipped into a pair of blue shorts. As she was reaching for her blouse, she saw the light blue T-shirt hanging on a hook inside her walk-in closet. It was Luke's. She'd borrowed it from him yesterday to help him paint the garage. Julianne picked up the paint-speckled shirt and lifted it to her face to smell the faint scent of Luke's cologne she knew was present. Her eyes misted with tears.

She loved him. Deeply.

She even loved wearing that old shirt. It made her feel close to him, almost a part of him. That was what she wanted to be. Luke's partner in life, his helpmate, his wife...but instead Luke was breaking her heart and probably didn't even know it.

She pulled the shirt on over her head and tugged her hair free to let it fall around her shoulders. Maybe that was the problem. Luke needed to know how she felt? How much she'd grown to love him? Could she be that straightforward? Could she tell the man she was completely, totally crazy about him? In love in a way she'd never known before now? Yes, she could do that, she thought as she studied her reflection in the mirror. Then her eyes lowered to her waistline. She could give Luke all the love her heart had to offer, but she still couldn't give him a child. Craig Johnson had regarded that as intolerable, unthinkable. Enough to walk away from all their plans. Enough to leave her. Forever. Maybe Luke O'Hara found that equally unattractive. She winced at the thought. He had Nora and Todd. *They* had Nora and Todd. Couldn't that be enough for him if it was enough for Julianne? She wouldn't know the answers unless she asked questions.

Julianne turned to head down the staircase and into the kitchen. Filling a cup with water, she slid it into the microwave. A cup of tea. That's what helped her to unwind after a stressful day at the center, although she doubted it would perform any miracles for her today. A tea bag came easily out of the red canister when Julianne pulled on it. Soon she plopped it into a steaming cup of water. She had no more than discarded the tea bag and added honey to her hot drink, when Luke walked in the kitchen door. Alone.

"Where are the kids?" she asked.

"Still with the baby-sitter," he replied. "Are you okay?"

She nodded.

He motioned toward a kitchen chair. "Will you sit down and talk with me for a few minutes?"

Julianne nervously cleared her throat and turned away from him, reaching for a spoon on the counter. "Let me stir this first. Would you like some tea?"

"No, thank you. I'm not much of a tea drinker."

"I know," she said softly without turning to face him. What did he think? That she didn't know the million little things about him that she'd learned these past few weeks. Like his favorite color. His least favorite movies. His preferred beverage. "Tea isn't what you're used to, Luke, but that doesn't mean you wouldn't like it. Does it?" She swiveled around slowly to see his curious expression.

He studied her lifted eyebrows, the doubtful, hesitant look in her eyes and wondered if there was something important in her words that he was missing. "No, I guess not. Would you make a cup for me?" He watched her eyes brighten as if at some small victory she'd apparently won that he didn't understand.

Julianne reached into the cupboard for another cup to fill with water. In only a moment, she had the microwave running again, and Luke was still standing in the doorway, watching her. Loving her.

"Julianne," he began quietly. "Why are you here, now, in this kitchen when you could be at the wedding reception celebrating Rachel and Morgan's marriage?"

"I couldn't stay there any longer, Luke. Beautiful brides, lovely weddings, probably a bouncing baby boy in their future." Her eyes filled with tears. "I couldn't take any more of it."

Luke realized she'd seen what he'd seen this afternoon. Mrs. Rachel Talbot. A bride whose shining eyes had spoken of the love she felt for her new husband more than any words could convey. That's what he'd cheated Julianne out of. A marriage like that. A commitment to a man she wanted to be committed to—not to a family, a situation, a need to be met. Luke moved toward her, wanting to take her gently into his arms and hold her, ease her sadness; but she shook her head when his hands touched her shoulders.

"Don't, Luke. You'll make it too easy for me to cry."

"Sometimes crying is the only thing left to do," he remarked in a weary voice and gathered her into his arms. She leaned into him, fighting back a sob, as he added, "Lord knows, I've done enough of it to last me a lifetime."

But never over me, she wanted to shout at him. Never over me. She buried her face against his chest and wept. All the while, Luke held her close. "It's okay, Julianne. Things will be okay," he whispered to her. He desperately wanted to make everything okay for her, but he had no idea if he had that power within him. He couldn't make her love him the way he loved her. There was no happy ending guaranteed for what he'd done by marrying a bright, beautiful young woman at a time in his life when his soul had barely an ounce of feeling left in it. She'd deserved so much better than what he'd offered.

Finally, when the crying subsided, Julianne lifted her head to look up into her husband's questioning gaze. "I'm almost too ashamed to admit this to you, but I was jealous, unbelievably jealous of Betty and Warren's engagement announcement...and of Rachel."

Luke hugged her to him again, pressing his mouth against her warm temple. "I'm sorry you didn't have a big wedding like Rachel's. We should have waited.''

"No," she interrupted and wiped her eyes with a tissue she'd pulled from her pocket. "It wasn't the wedding, Luke. It was the love. The way Rachel looked at Morgan; the way he looked at her. And it was the same with Betty and Warren. They're crazy about each other, and I'm so jealous I can hardly stand it. And, believe me, I know how selfish that sounds."

"It's not selfish to want to be madly in love with the person you marry," he said with a sigh. "Under ordinary circumstances, that's pretty much a given." He hesitated as he considered the many things she'd missed by agreeing to marry a man she didn't love. He hadn't meant to take anything away from her. "Maybe marrying first and then hoping love would follow wasn't the best idea in the world."

"Maybe not," she agreed quietly. "But it's not too late for us, is it?" She gave a sad laugh. "I mean, we're still newlyweds by most people's standards. Oh, Luke..." She leaned her forehead against his shoulder, melting into the warmth of his comforting embrace. "I know you need this marriage to work. I don't want to disappoint you."

"Nothing about you could ever disappoint me." But icy fear gripped Luke's heart even as he spoke. He was losing her. And he'd have to let her go. He loved her too much to try to make her spend her life with a husband she didn't love. "But I don't want you to be sad like this." He whispered the words as he held her, his mouth moving against her silky hair.

Then he spoke her name and pulled slightly away. "Julianne, look at me. Please." His hands sifted through blond curls, turning her face up to his. He winced at the sight of her watery eyes. Something he'd caused. It reminded him of her tears that first time they'd kissed. He wished he'd kept right on kissing her that night instead of foolishly ending something that had been just what he needed. This woman's love. "Julianne…" He started speaking, with every intention of telling her he'd let her go if that's what she wanted. But he kept thinking of that first kiss. She had wanted it, too. And it hadn't felt like a first kiss. It had seemed like it was meant to be. That's what had scared him. How could that happen to them—to anyone—so quickly? How could he feel that way with Julianne? After spending only a year alone? That's where the guilt had come from in those early days of knowing her. But his guilt was gone now, and he wished they could go back in time, back to their beginnings, to that moment of pure longing, one for the other. Luke's gaze lowered to the sad downward curve of her mouth. Maybe they could. Maybe he could take her there. "Julianne," he spoke quietly, hesitantly. "Do you remember the first time we kissed?"

Julianne sniffed and nodded. Yes, she remembered, as well as he did.

"Let's go back there." He watched her eyes register uncertainty at his suggestion, but his own uncertainty was gone.

She tilted her head a little to one side in question. "But how can we?" she asked as her heart thudded loudly within her breast. A thousand sensations shivered through her as Luke raised a hand to gently touch her face. He brushed a warm thumb across her slightly parted lips, and his darkening blue eyes, brimming with emotion, held her gaze steady.

"Like this," Luke said in a faltering voice as he slowly, deliberately lowered his mouth to hers, their hearts meeting in a kiss that was as necessary to their survival as air to breathe. Julianne relaxed easily into the strong arms that encircled her, and Luke drew her closer into the embrace as naturally as if she'd been created to be there.

"Luke," she barely whispered his name when he abandoned the sweet taste of her lips to brush his mouth against her forehead, her eyes, the tip of her nose. "Luke, don't—"

He raised his head instantly with unspeakable hurt in the depths of his eyes. "Don't kiss you?"

Julianne shook her head and smiled at his misunderstanding. "Don't stop. Ever."

His smile warmed her heart before he silenced her request with his mouth meeting hers, moving firmly against its softness. Then, the lingering exchange that had begun with tenderness, deepened rapidly. Julianne slipped her arms around his neck and let her fingers slide into soft brown hair as she returned her husband's possessive kiss with more longing than she'd ever known. Then Luke slowly raised his head far enough away from her to whisper the words she feared she might never hear from him—words that only made her want him more.

"I love you, Julianne."

A cry of joy burst from her and her eyes flew open. "Oh, Luke, are you sure? I mean, I'm so in love with you I can't think straight anymore." She placed her hands on his chest, feeling his pounding heart beneath her palms.

"You love me?" he asked, mystified by her words. "But I thought the reason you were so sad was because you didn't love me the way Rachel loves her husband or Betty loves Warren…that you were missing out on that part of life."

"No, no, no." She shook her head and laughed, blissfully happy with his revelation. "I've been so sad because I was sure you'd never love me, never want me the way I want you."

Luke stared at her, clearly stunned by her admission. "Not love you? Not want you? What have I done to make you think that?"

"Nothing," she said, suddenly serious.

"But I must have done something—"

"No, Luke. It's what you didn't do," she stated softly. "You didn't seem to want to be alone with me, you didn't touch me or hold me."

"Julianne, you're so young. You've never been in a relationship like this. I didn't want you to feel like I was pressuring you."

"But I'd never think that about you."

"That's part of the problem. I didn't know what you thought about me, how you felt about me." He paused, carefully considering the words he really longed to say. "I know that you love my children. That's obvious. But as for me, I haven't been certain what you felt. I didn't want you to feel some wrong sense of duty or obligation. I wouldn't expect that. Julianne, I want you to love me, to want me, too," he explained as he studied the beautiful brown eyes that sparked with new life.

"And I've been waiting for you to move first, speak first, do something, Luke. Anything. I wanted to believe there was something to hope for between us. I thought maybe, since I can't give you more children, maybe you might find that unattractive. Maybe you wouldn't want me."

"Not want you?" He hugged her tightly. "The challenge is not to want you every minute of the day." Then he looked into her questioning eyes. "I love you, Julianne. Forever. Whether or not we have a child together has nothing to do with my feelings for you. Nora and Todd are enough for me, and I'm hoping they'll be enough to satisfy you."

"Oh, Luke, I love those kids. They make me so very happy," she admitted and hugged him back in relief. "And if it weren't for them, I wouldn't have you in my life, in my heart."

Luke smiled and kissed her forehead gently, speaking warm words against her skin. "I love you, Julianne. I've loved you for a long time, but I didn't realize it until we went to see Maggie at the hospital last night. And I've prayed nearly every moment since then, thanking God for sending you to me, for the blessing you are in my life…and asking Him for your love."

Julianne was momentarily speechless. Those were the sweetest words she'd heard spoken. By anyone. Ever. "Praying? About me?" She was smiling and radiant, and Luke's mouth curved with tenderness as he gazed into her hopeful eyes.

"Yes," he replied before his hand touched her face again. "I want you to be my wife because you love me, Julianne. Not for any other reason."

She raised a hand to touch his, pressing it to her cheek. "I do love you, Luke. Very much," she said and gently turned her head to press her mouth against his palm in a light kiss.

From the intensity of his gaze, she thought he would kiss her again, but he did not. Instead he took her hand in his, linking his fingers through hers and giving an easy tug. "Come with me."

They walked from the kitchen into the living room, toward the rolltop desk they rarely used that sat in the corner of the room. "There's something in here that belongs to you." He pulled open the middle drawer and took a small jeweler's box from it. The gray velvet brushed softly against her hand as he placed it there. "Open it."

Julianne snapped open the lid to find a brilliant diamond solitaire ring nestled inside more velvet. "Luke, this is beautiful. It's lovely." She raised her eyes to see him watching her, smiling with a tenderness in his eyes that she knew belonged to her.

"I bought it this morning. I wanted something to give you, something to mark a new beginning when the time was right. Something to express how much I love you, Julianne." He lifted the box from her hand and removed the engagement ring. He slid it onto her finger where it fit snugly up against her shiny gold wedding band.

"It fits perfectly, Luke. And it matches our wedding rings."

"I know," he responded. "I went back to the same jeweler to find one that would match." He looked from the sparkling diamond into Julianne's eyes, shining and bright. "I promise to love you, Julianne, for as long as I live. Will you marry me? Again?"

She was so surprised, she could do no more than nod at first, her brown eyes wide in amazement. "Are you serious, Luke? A second ceremony?"

"Yes. Reverend Hunter will do the honors this time. He's already agreed."

She blinked. "You've asked him?"

"Right after I bought the ring. I thought that, maybe, if Ben had a ceremony for us, you'd feel more officially married."

"That's a lovely idea, Luke," she replied, "honestly, but..." Her heart quickened its pace in the awkward silence. How could she express what she wanted him to understand? Her cheeks warmed in an unwelcome blush as she looked into his darkening eyes for a long moment. "I don't need another wedding to make our marriage feel official, Luke." She hesitated. "I need you."

"You have me," he responded. His smile was warm, intimate as he gathered her into his arms, his steady gaze never leaving hers. He could get lost in the way she looked at him, and lost someplace with this woman was precisely where he wanted to be. For the remainder of his life. "Julianne..." He spoke tender words, whispering in her hair as he pulled her close. "Reverend Hunter offered to keep the kids overnight...so we can have some time alone."

A small, shy smile barely touched Julianne's lips. She settled snugly into her husband's strong arms to enjoy the feel of his hands against the hollow of her back. "Good. Tell him we need as much time as he'll give us."

Luke smiled and hugged her tighter. "No more nights of sleeping alone in the room across the hall. I want you by my side. Always." He tipped his head to look into her eyes. "You've shown me that I do believe in miracles, Julianne. Your love for me is one of them."

She raised up, inviting his kiss, and the love she saw shining in the clear blue depths of Luke's gaze was for her and her alone. And for that, she would thank the Lord. Profusely. Later.

Epilogue

The same village green that held the Strawberry Festival followed by Rachel and Morgan Talbot's wedding reception, soon held the Arts and Crafts Fair in mid-September. The O'Haras were among the many families, young and old alike, who spent their Saturday strolling through the green. They looked at different exhibits and craft displays as well as played games with the kids. The music that filled the air was provided alternately by local gospel talent and the high school concert band.

Nora's and Todd's faces were quickly painted up like Native Americans by a church group earning money for next year's summer camp. Nora was a princess, or so she believed, while Todd was a young warrior, beating his chest and pretending to shoot arrows at his sister. Finally, Luke and Julianne had to separate them, one on either side of an adult, to keep Nora from clobbering Todd to get even for being shot at repeatedly.

Julianne just laughed, but Luke was relieved when Reverend Ben showed up and offered to take the children for story time at the library's booth set up on the north side of the green.

"Whew, what a nice break," Luke remarked as he watched the trio, Reverend Ben flanked on both sides by a skipping child, walk away.

"He looks right at home with them, doesn't he?" Julianne commented. She slipped her arm through her husband's and leaned her head against his shoulder. "Wow, a few minutes to ourselves. What do you think we should do first?"

"Find a private place to kiss," he answered, drawing more soft laughter from his wife, and his mouth curved into a generous grin. "Ben said he'd keep the kids until 4:00 p.m. I always knew Reverend Hunter was a good man."

"He's a good man whether or not he baby-sits our children, my dear."

"True, but that's worth some extra points. Don't you think?"

"Luke, look. There's the stand where Betty and Warren are selling homemade candy. Let's buy a box for Maggie. She loves peanut butter fudge." Julianne pulled away from Luke to reach into her skirt pocket for some money.

"I know someone else who loves peanut butter fudge," he said and leaned forward to kiss her lightly on the mouth. "You'd better buy a box for yourself, too, Mrs. O'Hara."

Julianne smiled and raised a hand to touch Luke's

face. "I like your kisses better. They're much sweeter…and they're free," she said quietly.

"All right, all right. Break it up, you two lovebirds," came a man's voice from behind them.

They turned to see Frank directly behind them. "You've been married long enough not to act like that in public," he teased.

"You're just jealous because your wife isn't here with you," Luke responded. "How is Maggie, anyway?"

"Bored with at least another month off work until the baby arrives."

"Once the little fellow is born, Maggie will never have to worry about being bored again." Luke's arm moved around Julianne's waist and held her close to his side as he spoke.

"True enough," Frank answered. "I'm here on a mission right now. I'm supposed to buy peanut butter fudge and an order of barbecued chicken from the booth the Parent-Teacher Association is running. I have to keep Mom-to-be happy, you know. That's my number one purpose in life for the next four weeks."

Luke and Julianne waved goodbye and watched their brother-in-law disappear into the crowd.

"I don't think of Maggie as a mom-to-be. Do you?" Julianne asked as they continued to walk in the direction Frank had taken.

"I hadn't really thought about it one way or the other," Luke replied with a shrug.

"But she's already a mom. I mean, I'll bet she

feels like one, today, right this very minute, with a baby living and moving inside her."

Luke didn't answer. He hadn't given much thought to Julianne's feelings about Maggie's pregnancy, but it occurred to him, now, how difficult that must be for her considering her own inability to conceive a child. Maybe this would be a good time to mention the discussion he had with the twins earlier that day. He had planned to tell her tonight at home, but right now felt right. "Julianne, the kids asked me something this morning, and I need to find out what you think about their request."

"What request?"

An expression of satisfaction brightened Luke's gaze. "Nora and Todd both wanted to know if they could start calling you mommy." He waited for the smile he expected his announcement to bring to her lips, but it didn't come. Instead, she glanced away from him, catching her lower lip between her teeth in a nervous movement. "Julianne, I thought that would make you happy," he stated honestly.

"I'm happy that they love me enough to want to call me that, but I'm not sure that it would be fair to Kimberly."

They continued walking through the crowd of people for a moment in silence. Julianne was lost in deep thought while Luke searched for an appropriate response to give. When they neared the north side of the green, he reached for her hand and directed her toward The Old First Church.

"Luke, where are we going?"

"Over there to the park benches at the side of the

church. I want a few minutes alone with you," he replied and within moments, they were seated on a wooden bench away from the noisy crowd they'd emerged from. "Julianne," he began as he looked down at her slender hand. The rings that she wore on her left hand gleamed shiny and new in the mid-afternoon sunlight. "Nora and Todd love you. They want you to be their mother. They want to feel like your children."

"I love them, too, Luke, probably more than you even understand, but...Kimberly was their mother. She gave them life. She's the one that deserves that title. I don't think it would be fair for me to claim it."

Luke chose his words carefully. "I think you're more than fair to Kimberly. Her picture still sits on the dresser in the kids' room."

"As it should," Julianne added. "They need to remember her."

Luke nodded in agreement. "But I hear you answer their questions about her at times, and I know there are nights when you go through that old family album with them, showing them photos of her with them when they were babies and then toddlers. That can't be easy for you." Luke spoke with a tinge of wonder in his voice. Her willingness to give the twins' mother such a significant place in their lives continually amazed him. As did his deepening love for Julianne. He'd thought many times he couldn't love a woman more than he loved this one, but now he found himself loving her more today than he did yesterday. The depth of love that God had granted them seemed endless.

Luke's voice became a little unsteady as he continued. "Last night I heard you tell Nora that her hair would be a beautiful auburn someday. Just like her mother's was."

"I told her it's a gift from Kimberly," Julianne added quietly, watching Luke raise her hand to his mouth and brush a kiss against her soft fingers.

"And the smiles I see on my children's faces every day are a gift from you, Julianne. You make them happy, you make them feel special and loved in a way only you can."

Julianne's eyes glistened with tears. "If it weren't for Kimberly, I wouldn't have any children to love, to share my life with, Luke. I can't have a baby with you, no matter how badly I want one, but with Nora and Todd, I feel like a mom. How do I thank Kimberly for that?" She leaned her head against her husband's shoulder. "How do you thank someone for giving something like that?"

"By being the mother the kids need. By letting them have a mommy here that they can see and touch and love." He kissed the top of her head. "Julianne, if I loved you any more than I already do, I'm not sure my heart could stand it."

She laughed softly and raised her head to study his face unhurriedly. "I know what you mean, Luke. I feel the same about you." Leaning forward, she touched her mouth against his, inviting the sweet tenderness of his kiss for a lingering moment. Then she whispered words she'd not spoken before today.

"There isn't anything in this life I want more than to have your baby. I even dream about it at night." She lowered her sad gaze to her rings.

Luke's hand moved to her chin, and he tilted her face up, forcing her to meet his eyes. "I want you to see another doctor. An infertility expert. Get a second opinion, maybe a third or fourth. Whatever it takes until we know for sure."

"There's probably not much chance that my gynecologist could be wrong. She sounded very sure of herself when she explained the situation to me."

"We can't take the word of just one physician on something this important. We need to find out more," he urged in a gentle voice. "And we should definitely keep trying, however long it takes," he said with just a hint of a smile.

Julianne smiled and slipped an arm around his waist. "Let's go home, Luke."

"Yes, let's do exactly that," he replied, and they started walking together toward the house that God's love had turned into a home.

*   *   *   *   *

If you enjoyed Kathryn Alexander's
TWIN WISHES,
join the Fairweather folks
next month in:
BEN'S BUNDLE OF JOY,
by Lenora Worth
On sale April 2000
Don't miss it!

Dear Reader,

Isn't it wonderful how God so many times rescues us from our own mistakes? Julianne Quinn takes a big risk in this book when she marries Luke O'Hara, a man who has turned his back on God. As Reverend Ben Hunter points out to Julianne during a counseling session, the Bible does not support the idea of a Christian entering into a marriage with a nonbeliever. It's Julianne's love for Luke's children that influences her to ignore her pastor's advice, and she agrees to the proposed marriage of convenience.

Fortunately for Julianne (and with a little help from this author), Luke O'Hara eventually returns to the Christian faith he'd abandoned. Kneeling in a small hospital chapel, Luke finally sees his need for the Lord in his life. Only then can a happy ending be enjoyed by all.

Thank you for choosing my book. It's been a pleasure to write this story for the Fairweather series. I hope you enjoy it!

Best wishes,

Kathryn Alexander

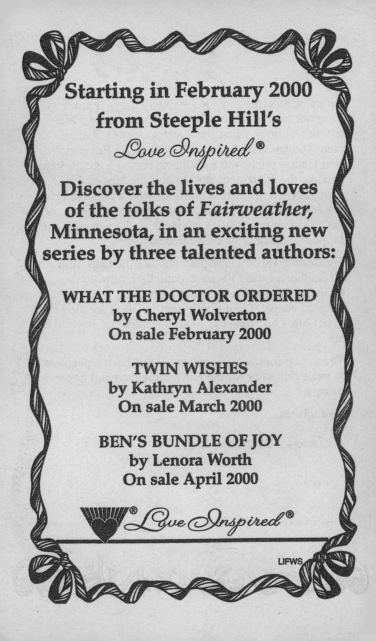

**Starting in February 2000
from Steeple Hill's**
Love Inspired ®

**Discover the lives and loves
of the folks of *Fairweather*,
Minnesota, in an exciting new
series by three talented authors:**

WHAT THE DOCTOR ORDERED
by Cheryl Wolverton
On sale February 2000

TWIN WISHES
by Kathryn Alexander
On sale March 2000

BEN'S BUNDLE OF JOY
by Lenora Worth
On sale April 2000

® *Love Inspired* ®

LIFWS

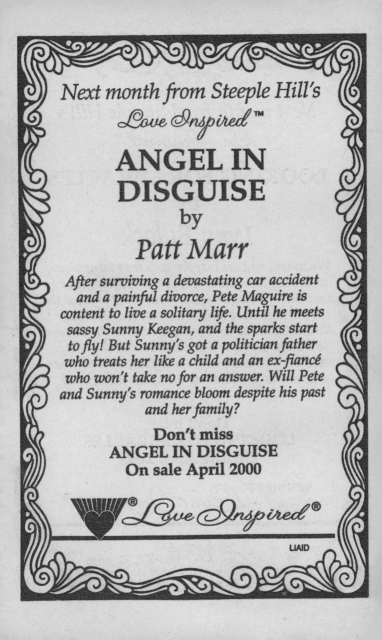